Marcie felt a rush of pain, remembering the heartbreak that had hit her so unexpectedly.

That was the worst part—the lack of warning. Her heart hurt afresh with the thought of Zack getting cold feet, of regretting he'd asked her to marry him.

"I heard you'd bought the café, and it sounded like you had things going your way. I knew you didn't want to leave Rocky Point. I did it all wrong," he said slowly. "I'm really sorry."

She stared at him for a long time, seeing the sincerity in his eyes. Her heart ached at the loss of the love they'd shared, at the dreams shattered. But life wasn't always fair. It didn't always go as she planned.

"So what now?" Zack asked.

"We go on, I guess. What else is there?"

"Can we be friends?"

Tears threatened. She'd loved him so much at one time and now all he wanted was to be friends. Swallowing hard, she nodded. "Sure, friends."

He reached out and took one of her hands in his. "More than friends?"

BARBARA McMAHON

was born and raised in the southern U.S., but settled in California after spending a year flying around the world for an international airline. She settled down to raise a family and work for a computer firm, and began writing when her children started school. Now, feeling fortunate in being able to realize a long-held dream of quitting her day job and writing full-time, she and her husband have moved to the Sierra Nevada of California, where she finds her desire to write is stronger than ever. With the beauty of the mountains visible from her windows, and the pace of life slower than that of the hectic San Francisco Bay Area, where they previously resided, she finds more time than ever to think up stories and characters and share them with others through writing. Barbara loves to hear from readers. You can reach her at P.O. Box 977, Pioneer, CA 95666-0977. Readers can also contact Barbara at her website, www.barbaramcmahon.com.

Rocky Point Reunion
Barbara McMahon

Love Inspired

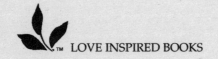 LOVE INSPIRED BOOKS

Recycling programs
for this product may
not exist in your area.

ISBN-13: 978-0-373-81552-4

ROCKY POINT REUNION

Copyright © 2011 by Barbara McMahon

All rights reserved. Except for use in any review, the reproduction
or utilization of this work in whole or in part in any form by any
electronic, mechanical or other means, now known or hereafter
invented, including xerography, photocopying and recording, or in
any information storage or retrieval system, is forbidden without
the written permission of the editorial office, Love Inspired Books,
233 Broadway, New York, NY 10279 U.S.A.

This is a work of fiction. Names, characters, places and incidents are
either the product of the author's imagination or are used fictitiously, and
any resemblance to actual persons, living or dead, business establishments,
events or locales is entirely coincidental.

This edition published by arrangement with Love Inspired Books.

® and TM are trademarks of Love Inspired Books, used under license.
Trademarks indicated with ® are registered in the United States Patent
and Trademark Office, the Canadian Trade Marks Office and in other
countries.

www.LoveInspiredBooks.com

Printed in U.S.A.

See, I have written your name
on the palms of my hands.
—*Isaiah* 49:16

To dear friends Patti and Renee.
What wonderful friendship we share.
Thanks for all the support over the years.

Chapter One

The wind blew from the sea, keeping the early summer temperature comfortable. Marcie Winter had her arms full, boxes of hot dog buns stacked precariously beneath her chin, plastic bags of hot dogs ready to cook dangling from her fingers. She paused for breath at the top of the small dune and smiled when she saw the crowd on the beach. It was a good turnout. Yet how could it not be? The first church picnic of the summer and with gorgeous weather.

Two portable barbecues had already been set up. Trestle tables had been erected nearby—already laden with the potluck fare. Children swarmed around, laughing and shouting and chasing each other in makeshift games of tag. An impromptu game of volleyball was in play and younger children were piling damp sand for castles, watched over by mothers and older siblings.

It was the annual Trinity Church picnic and everyone was expected.

Slowly she half walked, half slid down the four-foot dune, arriving on the flat sand without mishap. In moments she relinquished her packages to willing hands.

"Need any help?" one of the mothers asked as Marcie stacked the boxes of rolls near the barbecue.

"I'm good. One more trip will do it," Marcie said, already hurrying across the sand. It was easier going without balancing things. She couldn't wait to kick off her sandals and walk barefoot on the sand. But not until she'd finished with the gravel parking lot.

As she reached her car, a familiar truck turned into the space three down from her. Catching her breath, Marcie couldn't move for a moment. She felt as if time stood still. It was Joe Kincaid's truck. But he couldn't be driving. Joe was out of town.

It had to be Zack. After ten long years.

She knew Zack was in town. How could she not when she owned the only café in town? No one needed a newspaper in Rocky Point, Maine. They only had to come for coffee, pie—and a bit of town gossip. But no one mentioned he'd be at the picnic. He'd come back to help out at home when his brother burned his hands. What was he doing here?

Marcie held her breath as the passenger door of

the pickup opened. She released it when his niece, Jenny jumped out, calling a greeting to Marcie. Her young voice broke the spell. Marcie called back a hello and opened the trunk of her car for the condiments and plastic cups she was also contributing— *and* to shield her for a moment while she regained her composure. She hoped fervently that Zack was only dropping Jenny off for the picnic. *Please, Lord,* she prayed. *Don't let him stay.*

"Auntie Marcie, we're here for the picnic!" Jenny called out and ran over to her, hugging her around the waist. "It didn't rain!"

"No, it's a beautiful day," Marcie said, giving her a quick hug, keeping her back to the truck. She smiled at the young girl whom she'd known from birth. Jenny was seven years old and so full of life she brought a lot of joy to Marcie's life. The child's mother had died when she was two. Her dad was engaged to Gillian, a new friend of Marcie's, and she wished they were the ones bringing Jenny to the picnic. But they were in Las Vegas, closing Gillian's apartment, preparing for her move to Rocky Point, Maine.

Marcie heard footsteps on the gravel and with each one, her heart seemed to beat faster. She'd tried for years to figure out what she'd do when and if she ever saw Zack Kincaid again. That moment had arrived and she still didn't have a clue.

"Marcie." He was silent for a few seconds, then added, "Need some help?"

She focused on Jenny, shocked at the wave of longing that swept through her at the sound of his voice. She hadn't heard it in ten years. If asked before this moment, she'd have said she'd be immune. But she wasn't. Hearing him swept her back to her carefree days when she thought they'd marry and live happily ever after. She clung to her composure with all she had, but mostly she wanted to cry—at their lost love, their forever gone chance at a life together. She felt his stare but refused to look at him.

"I can manage," she said, turning to pick up the last box, which held the industrial-size condiment containers and stacks of plastic cups.

"I'm gonna see if Sally Anne's here," Jenny said as she turned and began racing toward the low dunes that separated the beach from the parking lot.

"Marcie?"

"I'm surprised to see you here," she said, holding the box in front of her as a shield and finally turning to look at him. Zack Kincaid. Six feet tall and filled out more since she'd last seen him. Dark hair and dark eyes that had once held her enthralled. Her mind jumbled with images. He looked older, harder, different. He was not the same young man she'd known. But then—neither was she the same woman he'd once professed to love. She felt her heart catch, her breathing quicken. He still had that old charisma that had always made her happy in his presence. She did not want to be attracted to him. No, no, no!

"I brought Jenny."

His dark eyes held her gaze. Her heart beat erratically. She wished she could look away, but she was mesmerized—fascinated to see what the years had wrought. His brother Joe had kept her up-to-date on his career, even when she'd told him she wasn't interested. But hearsay wasn't the same. Zack looked fantastic. She almost groaned with the realization.

"I'll bring her home, you don't need to stay," she said brightly, wishing he'd vanish as he had before. Only this time her heart wouldn't be broken.

He turned those dark eyes on her. "Thanks, but I'd like to stay."

"I can't imagine why," she said, instantly regretting it. She snapped her mouth closed. It sounded petty. She was too flustered to think straight. Of course he'd want to come to the picnic. It was a community tradition and he'd missed so many. This would give him the perfect opportunity to see everyone and catch up a bit. She just wished the timing had been different. That she'd already brought the last box down and was surrounded by friends instead of caught off guard here in the parking lot.

Plus, she hadn't expected to feel anything but hurt and anger when she saw him again.

"Marcie, I'm sorry. Truly. If I could go back in time and change things, I would. I should have handled it differently—better." He looked contrite, but she dare not let herself forget for an instant the heartache his departure had caused. Not that she could forget the endless days of tears. The weeks and months of hoping he'd call or come back. Or at least write. Still, it lay in the past. She wanted it to stay in the past, to not have to deal with the pain and sadness that she'd experienced before. They'd been in love, planning a life together. It had ended. There was nothing more to do but move on. "I guess there's no good way to say goodbye," she said, turning and walking toward the beach.

The wide sandy preserve was perfect for the annual beginning-of-summer picnic. She'd been attending ever since she'd been a child.

Without warning, he lifted the box out of her arms. "I'll carry this."

"I can manage," she said through gritted teeth. She didn't want to be around this man. He'd broken her heart a decade ago. Where she had once thought they'd attend Trinity picnics together for years, this was his first since he'd left her at the altar.

For a moment she considered wrestling the box

from him. Or dashing to her car and leaving. But too many people had already seen her, and the last thing she wanted was to give rise to the speculation and gossip that had plagued her so much in the past. Raising her head, she silently vowed to brazen it out. She just hoped Zack would stay as far from her as possible.

"I'm home for a while," he said.

"How nice for you," she replied. Where was a friend when she needed one? If only someone would beckon her over. Or call with an emergency at the café that she'd have to attend to personally.

"You're looking good," he said, easily keeping pace with her on the shifting sand.

She stopped at the top of the dune and turned, glaring at him. "Let's get one thing clear, Zack. You left. You made your choice, so don't come back here and try to make nice. Stay out of my way and I'll stay out of yours."

With that she stomped down the incline and headed straight for the water. Let him deliver the condiments. She was almost shaking in reaction. Tears blurred her vision as she stared at the sea. She'd loved him to bits and he'd shattered her heart when he'd left with no warning, nothing but a phone call the night before they were to marry. She'd spent the past ten years moving on. She had a nice life now. She did! She did not need Zack Kincaid coming home and causing complications.

* * *

Zack watched her move across the sand, unable to take his eyes off her. She'd always been the most graceful thing he'd ever seen. She was still a petite bundle of energy. Her long brown hair was pulled back, showing off her dark eyes and pretty complexion. Clearly highlighting the anger in her gaze.

Once she'd looked at him as if he'd hung the moon. Now she wanted nothing to do with him. He'd caught a glimpse of the hurt in her eyes. He'd done that. To someone he'd loved. He felt lower than low. He needed to make things better between them.

What did he expect? He'd caused the breach. Deliberately and without thinking things through. It had haunted him all these years. In the early days he'd fantasized that he'd return home for her and she'd be waiting. That he'd sweep her off her feet and take her with him, despite her avowal when they were growing up that she never wanted to live anywhere but Rocky Point.

He'd dreamed that she had accepted his apology and forgiven him. That dream evaporated. She was still angry. She had every right to be. But he had hoped.

He carried the box to the food area, conscious of the stares and whispers as people recognized him. It had been a mistake coming today. He'd resisted, but his niece had wanted to come so badly, he'd acquiesced. Now he wished he'd made arrangements for someone else to bring her.

"Zack Kincaid? Hey, I didn't know you were visiting," a friend from his school days greeted him. Instantly two other people joined them.

"Zack, back for a visit?" the woman asked. He recognized her but couldn't recall her name.

"I can't believe you're back, man," another old friend said. "You haven't been back in years. Call me, we'll get together for a coffee or something."

"Hey, Zack, good to see you!" Pete Marin came over and took the box. Several others called a greeting. He should have expected it, he thought as he nodded to those who called. Everyone knew everyone in Rocky Point. "I heard you were back in town," Pete said. "We missed you in church this morning. You'll have to come next Sunday." Pete's easy manner helped Zack get his bearings. There were others in town besides Marcie Winter. And he'd been avoiding them all since he'd been back. For no good reason now. Everyone seemed genuinely pleased to see him. He'd have to stop being a hermit if he was serious about moving back home.

"Good to see you, Pete. What have you been up to?" Zack asked.

He listened as Pete talked about his accounting business, but Zack's mind was on Marcie. Shifting slightly, he could see her standing at the water's edge. She looked so alone.

Zack nodded where appropriate, impatient to leave and go to the water's edge. A couple of others called a greeting. He smiled and gave a short wave. Plenty of time to catch up on what others were doing. If he stayed. Which was the plan.

He took the cola someone offered, chatted a moment with two other men he'd known as a teenager, then headed where he'd wanted to go since he chased her away. Marcie stood a dozen yards or so to his left. Should he try again?

Suddenly Jenny and several of her friends ran over to Marcie and soon all the little girls were talking a mile a minute. He'd wait.

Marcie looked up and straight at him. She didn't acknowledge him and quickly turned back to the girls.

It was no more than he deserved, but it hurt. He wanted to make things right. Barring that, he at least wanted peace between them. He'd messed up big-time. There wasn't much excuse for it, either. Ten years ago he'd seen a chance for his dream and taken it. Never looked back. Ever since he could remember he'd wanted to race cars. He'd done his fair share around Rocky Point, mostly illegally. When the opportunity had turned up, he'd gone for it. Only, he didn't realize until later the true cost of that decision.

He'd looked back plenty of times and never seen the way to regain her trust. At the time he'd thought the decision best. Hers and his. He hadn't wanted to tie her to a man who was racing in Europe. She never wanted to leave Rocky Point. He'd wanted to go. Could they have reached some kind of compromise? Now he was home. He'd missed her for ten solid years. Never found another person he related to as he and Marcie had when they were teenagers, planning their lives together. He had not come back with the hope of regaining her trust or her love. He figured he'd shattered that for all time. If he had the chance to do it over, he'd handle it differently.

Taking a breath, he started walking toward her. If anything was to change, he'd have to start it. He hoped he'd find the right words.

Marcie glanced again across the short distance of beach and her heart stopped, then began to race. Zack was heading her way. His dark brown eyes narrowed as he focused solely on her. His strong jaw signaled determination and resolve. What was he coming to say? Another attempt at apology? It was way too late for that.

What she really wanted was an *explanation* that would erase the pain and hurt of the past and give her understanding of why he'd done what he'd done. Except she knew that answer already and it never helped.

She took a breath and focused on the girls around her, hoping he'd take the hint and stay away. He'd been back for several weeks, but he picked this picnic as the first time they'd meet. Why? Why had he waited? Why hadn't he sought her out before?

"Uncle Zack," Jenny called. "Come and help us."

Marcie sighed softly. It seemed as if everything was against her today. She kept her gaze firmly on the girls from Jenny's class.

"What's going on?" Zack asked as he joined them.

"We want to go swimming, but the water's too cold," Jenny said.

"Can you think up a way so we stay warm while swimming?" another little girl asked.

Marcie smiled and shook her head. "There is no way, sweetie. You'll all just need to wait a few more weeks and it'll be closer to swimming weather."

"But we want to go today!"

Zack gave the girl a sympathetic smile. "Marcie's right. The water's too cold. How about you find something else to do by the water, but not in it. Like, who can throw a stick the farthest," he suggested, remembering back when he'd been their age and his father had coaxed Joe and him to try that, rather than risk hypothermia by going into the water.

"We don't have any sticks," one girl said.

He looked up to the high-water line on the sand. "I bet you can find them. Tell you what, I'll judge the distance if you each bring five sticks."

With a shout the girls dashed up the beach toward the high-water mark.

Marcie looked at him. "You handled that nicely." With a smile she turned and walked toward the tables of food.

He started to follow when Jenny ran back, clutching an assortment of sticks.

Giving in to his niece, he knew he'd have to exercise more patience than he wanted, and waited for the other girls to return. In addition to making things right with Marcie, he wanted to know his niece better. He was practically a stranger to her. It was his own fault, but he was back to make amends.

As the afternoon wore on, Zack became more and more frustrated. Every time he approached Marcie, she'd find something to do or someone to talk to that excluded him. She and one woman seemed to spend a lot of time together. She looked familiar, probably a friend from high school. The name would come to him. In the meantime he talked to other old friends, listened to Pastor John's pitch about attending church again and played a couple of games of beach volleyball to expend some of the frustration that was building.

At one point he conceded that she had every right

to make his penance harder by not cooperating. But he was determined. Sooner or later she'd have to talk with him. And then he hoped he could make her understand why he'd acted liked a dumb kid.

Zack and Tom Daggle, the town's mayor, were reminiscing when he heard his name spoken.

"Zack Kincaid?"

He turned to the teenager who'd walked up to them. He'd seen the boy earlier, a loner standing on the periphery of the crowd, never fully involved. Yet watching everyone as if not to miss a thing. "That's right."

"I'm Sean O'Connell." The boy held out his hand, looking nervous. He glanced at the mayor and nodded.

Zack shook it and nodded. "Nice to meet you, Sean."

"I heard you're a race car driver."

"Right again."

"Grand prix," Tom said. "Bringing fame to Rocky Point."

"Hardly," Zack said, amused. He was well-known on the grand prix circuit, having been in the winner's circle more times than not over the past few years. But grand prix racing wasn't as popular or as well-known in the States as in Europe.

"Better channeled that way than killing yourself or someone out on Ocean Side Avenue. Remember how much you liked driving fast? It was a miracle you didn't have a drawer full of speeding tickets," Tom said with a chuckle. "Do you remember you, me and Tate—?" The mayor looked at the teenager and changed his thought. "Not that we want anyone speeding around here these days."

Zack nodded in understanding. Not the thing to talk up around others, but he remembered racing down those three miles of straight road with Marcie cheering from the side. She'd been so supportive of his need for speed. Would she have waited if he'd asked her to? Instead, he'd broken off entirely with her to follow his dream. Not thinking at the time he was also shattering hers.

"Hey, man, you never crashed. Still haven't, have you?" Tom asked.

"You want to drive grand prix?" Zack asked.

"NASCAR, but I bet the techniques are similar," Sean said, with a wary look at the mayor.

"Probably. I could tell you a few things, I guess."

Sean looked around. "Not here. I know this isn't the place. But I heard you were in town and thought if I didn't ask you now, I might never run into you."

"I'm staying at Joe's place. His phone number's in the book. Give me a call," Zack said.

"Thanks." The teenager nodded again and walked away.

The two men watched him as he headed for the dunes and the parking lot.

"He's had a rough life," Tom said. "His dad left his mother—she's Earline Russell, Earline O'Connell now. She came back home to be with her folks and then her dad died. So it's Earline and her mother raising the boy."

"His father doesn't visit?"

"Disappeared. No one knows where he is. And he's not helping out financially. Watch Sean, though. He can be trouble."

Zack shrugged. "Can't be any worse than we were back when we were kids."

Tom laughed. "Good thing the fine folks in Rocky Point don't know all about that or I'd never have been elected mayor."

Zack glanced around casually and didn't see Marcie. He excused himself from the mayor and went to the table that held the drinks. Taking another can of soda, he looked around again. She was not on the beach. She must have left when he'd been talking with Tom. He took a long drink of the cold soda and realized all his interest in the picnic had fled.

They still needed to talk. Now the question was where and when. He wanted to convince her he was sorry.

And maybe see if there was anything left between them.

Chapter Two

Marcie stepped out of the bank and paused on the sidewalk, taking a moment to enjoy the beautiful June morning. The receipts from the weekend had been safely deposited. The lunch rush would not start for a couple of hours and she was free until then. Glancing at the colorful flowers spilling from the pots hanging from the old-fashioned wrought-iron lampposts, she smiled, happy in the day. She loved spring and summer the most. Maine weather was usually gorgeous in these seasons and she spent as much time outside as she could. The town looked its best at the beginning of summer, when visitors flooded the town, taking in the beautiful scenery, the boating and walks along the coast. And boosting her earnings at the café.

As she turned to head toward the café, she noticed Zack Kincaid across the road, talking with the sheriff. He hadn't seen her and it gave her a few minutes to study him as she'd been afraid to do at the picnic. How often had she wished things had turned out differently? Maturity gave her insight she'd lacked as a nineteen-year-old. Zack would never have been satisfied living in Rocky Point. He'd always wanted to travel, to see the world. To race. While she'd wanted a cottage by the sea with a white picket fence. How had they ever thought they'd have a chance at a long, happy marriage?

"Hello, Marcie, dear," Caroline Evans said as Marcie took a step and almost ran into the older woman.

She stopped abruptly and smiled at her older neighbor. "Hello, Caroline. Lovely day, isn't it?" She deliberately kept her back to the men across the street, hoping this conversation would be short and she could escape before Zack took it into his head to try to talk to her. After thinking about him nonstop since the picnic, she didn't trust herself around him just yet. She needed to gain some perspective, and not wonder if he still laughed at the same things she did. If he still liked pork barbecue more than anything else. If he could still stir feelings and longings she so wanted to ignore. Really, he'd said all she needed to hear at the beach yesterday.

"You looked deep in thought," Caroline commented. Glancing at the bank, she frowned. "Not money troubles, I hope."

"What? Oh, no, I just deposited the money from the weekend. Things are going very well." In that regard, at least.

"Hmm." Just then Caroline looked across the street. "Oh, dear," she murmured, looking back at Marcie with sympathy in her eyes.

"It's okay, it was a long time ago," Marcie said gently, hoping to forestall any expression of sympathy. Obviously Mrs. Evans hadn't heard of their meeting at the picnic. Marcie had had enough gossip and speculation ten years ago. Maybe the rumor mill would be more merciful this time.

"I have to get back to work. Have a great day, Caroline."

"You, too, dear. Don't let the past mar the present."

Marcie smiled and nodded. Good advice. She'd grieved enough over that lost love. She'd cried half an ocean when he'd left. Then she'd mopped up her tears, decided God had a different plan for her and she'd given herself over to whatever He decreed. The past decade had proved a blessing. She owned and operated her own restaurant, had moved out of her dad's home to a place of her own and had developed a strong network of friends.

Father God, you know how hard I've worked. Please let any meeting between us go smoothly. Don't let him wreak havoc with me again. I so need

Your peace and a little strengthening, Lord, she prayed as she walked along the sidewalk.

Her office was just off the kitchen, where she could easily keep an eye on things, jump in to help if needed or close the door and be alone. The Cabot sisters were busy switching from late breakfast orders to early lunch requests as Marcie gave a wave and continued to her desk.

Another blessing. The two older women, renowned for their cooking, had joined her nine years ago as cooks, and the excellent offerings from the kitchen, like their famous blueberry pie, rich and chunky potpies and corn beef dinners, kept locals and tourists coming day after day.

She ought to keep track of all her blessings, so numerous they should have crowded out the pain of Zack's leaving.

"Boss, we've got a problem with scheduling," Jessica said from the doorway.

Marcie turned from her computer and frowned as one of her longtime waitresses stepped into the office. Her uniform was an old-fashioned blue gingham dress with crisp white pinafore apron that added to the ambiance of the restaurant. Rocky Point had sent ships and sailors to the War for Independence, and some of the older structures in town dated prior to 1776. Marcie knew how to sell what tourists liked, and the old-fashioned atmosphere of the place suited both her and all the customers she could handle.

"And that would be what?" she asked, hoping for a major crisis to get her mind off Zack Kincaid.

"That new kid. He doesn't want to work Saturdays. He has other things to do, he says."

"I'll speak to him," Marcie said. "Ask him to see me, would you?"

"Thanks. He, um, is also a bit slow in doing things."

"Shirking?"

Jessica shrugged. She was not one to talk about other employees, so Marcie knew it was a bigger deal than Jessica was letting on if she'd seen fit to talk to her.

She needed something to get her mind off a certain man and back on track. Zack would be gone again soon and her peace would be restored.

The conversation didn't go as well as Marcie had hoped. He listened to her, but showed no emotion, and got up when she was finished and said he'd see what he could do. Not a ringing promise to do better in the future.

Midafternoon, Marcie was ready for a break. There was a lull in the customer traffic. One of the Cabot sisters had taken off and would return later. It was the perfect time to dash home and do a load of laundry.

"Auntie Marcie?" Jenny came rushing into her office, a big smile on her face.

"Hi, Jenny, what's up?" Marcie came from behind her desk to give the little girl a hug. Technically she was not Jenny's aunt. The marriage to her uncle Zack that would have cemented that relationship had not taken place. But Joe had insisted she be called aunt, as she was practically a member of the family. She liked to think she'd stepped up when Pamela had died and done all a real aunt would have done with Jenny. They spent a lot of time together. Now seven, Jenny was allowed to visit the restaurant on her own, as long as her father was in town. Or for now, her uncle.

"Uncle Zack said I could get a sundae. I'd like a chocolate fudge one, but only if you eat with me. Wasn't the picnic fun?"

"It was fun. Tell you what, I'm about to head for home to do some chores. We'll take the fixings and make our own deluxe hot fudge sundaes."

"I have my bike. I can ride to your place."

"Or walk over with me," Marcie suggested. "Check with your uncle to make sure that is all right. When we come back here later, your bike will be waiting." That way, Jenny could meet Zack out in front of the café and Marcie wouldn't have to see him.

Jenny had blossomed the past few months. Her mother had died in a car crash in which Jenny had been badly injured. Fortunately she'd been too young to remember it. Joe had been a very protective father until his elderly next-door neighbor died and her great-granddaughter showed up. Gillian joining the family was going to be a very good thing for Jenny. God would be at the center of Joe and Gillian's marriage and Marcie knew that gave it the best shot possible.

"My dad and Gillian called last night. They've sorted through all of Gillian's things and packed the rental truck. Daddy said they're going to clean the apartment really good today so they get back the 'posit and then come home. Did you know it will take days and days to drive home? I want to look at dresses."

Marcie smiled. "*Deposit,* Jenny. I did know it would take days to drive back here. I think they want to see some of the sights along the way, as well. And we can look at dresses online while we eat our sundaes if you like," Marcie said.

She'd clicked with Gillian as soon as the woman had come to town and couldn't wait for her new friend to return. She'd been asked to cater the wedding—and be a part of the bridal party. The big event would be the weekend after Labor Day, plenty of time for the plans to be finalized. She wanted the best for her new friend. In the meantime, Jenny had been given the task of picking out the bridesmaids' dresses. As a result she and Marcie had been poring over different ones on the internet. Jenny was thrilled to be the flower girl and loved to talk about the wedding.

"Why don't you call your uncle and make sure it's okay to go to my place," Marcie said, proud of the steadiness of her voice when mentioning Zack. She could do this!

Ten minutes later Marcie unlocked the door to the small apartment over the bakery. She'd rented it five years ago when she'd decided twenty-four was too old to be living at home. Actually, she'd decided that long before that year, but it had taken all her money to get her restaurant going. Finally able to afford this small apartment, she'd moved in and spent the past five years fixing it up to suit her. She had a view of Main Street, the aroma of fresh baked goods to awaken her and plenty of privacy when she wanted it.

Jenny carried the carton of ice cream, nuts, fudge and cherries they'd acquired from Marcie's café directly to the small kitchen that opened to the living space. Marcie quickly scooped the ice cream while the fudge heated in the microwave. Then she and Jenny heaped the delicious chocolate on the ice cream and dusted it with nuts.

"I'll put the cherries on," Jenny said, already dipping her fingers in the jar to pull out several. They had long ago decided one cherry was not enough.

Taking their concoctions to the small dining table, they began to eat.

"School will be over in three more days," Jenny said. "I wish they'd let us out before Memorial Day. We aren't learning anything anymore."

"Hey, kiddo, you can learn something new every day. What are you doing all day if not learning?"

"We're playing games." Jenny took a bite and let the ice cream slowly melt, then tilted her head. "But we have to use subtraction to solve some of the puzzles, or know the spelling of words to play Scrabble."

"Sounds like your teacher is applying all you learned this year while you have fun with the games," Marcie said.

Jenny's eyes grew wide.

"Are you winning games?" Marcie asked, smiling at Jenny's stunned realization.

"Yes. Sometimes. It's fun. But I still want school to be over. Then I can play with Sally Anne all day."

"Don't forget Vacation Bible School. It'll be right after Independence Day," Marcie said.

"I know, but that's different from regular school, more fun. And Sally Anne and I are in the same age group so we'll get to play together there. I hope Gillian's back by then. She's my teacher in Sunday school and said she wouldn't miss Vacation Bible School for anything."

"Then she'll be back. It doesn't take that long to drive here from Nevada. VBS is a month away, after all."

Jenny finished her ice cream, scraping the bowl until it was almost spotless. "And we'll have your snacks each day," she said.

Marcie nodded. She rose and took the bowls to rinse in the sink. "Healthful and nutritious." Because her schedule was erratic, Marcie couldn't teach at VBS, but she had been working on the snacks portion for several years. She loved being creative with cookie shapes and other snacks for the children.

Jenny laughed as she jumped up from the table. "But it's always good. We don't notice the nutritious part. Can we look at dresses now?"

Marcie smiled. "Sure, come on."

The next half hour passed quickly as they looked online at different gowns and dresses suitable for weddings. They were compiling a stack of printouts of dresses from different sites to review with Gillian when she returned. In the meantime, Marcie loved spending time with Jenny. Together they laughed at some dresses and grew seriously interested in a few.

When the knock sounded on the door, Marcie froze.

"That's Uncle Zack, I think," Jenny said. "He said I could come here until he picked me up. We're going to eat in Portland tonight. He's not much of a cook. But we have to finish printing this dress."

Marcie drew in a breath. The moment was at hand. She smiled at Jenny as she rose as if in a dream to go to the door. "You can wait until it finishes. I'll answer the door."

Opening it, she braced herself for the impact of seeing Zack up close again. When she saw him, time seemed to stand still. His smile had always been special; now she could see the man the boy she'd known had grown into. It still had the power to knock her sideways.

"Hello, Marcie," he said easily.

Surprisingly, a polite smile came without much effort. "Jenny's just about ready." She clung to the door, hoping her pounding heart wasn't evident to the man standing on the landing. She wished they were back in high school. She'd fly out to meet him. Instead, everything had changed. They were practically strangers now.

"I had to ask where you lived. No one was home at your parents' house."

"I've lived here for five years now," she said. Which he would have known if he'd kept up with her at all. It hurt to realize he had not. Surely his brother would have mentioned at some point what she was doing. Had Zack never asked after her? She had tried to resist when Joe spoke about him, but had gleaned information as the years had passed.

"Over the bakery? Doesn't it get noisy?"

"Sometimes in the early morning. But it suits me." Though it was nothing like the clapboard house they'd talked about living in, complete with white picket fence. But then, nothing was as they'd talked about before.

"I'm ready, Uncle Zack," Jenny said, coming to the door carrying a stack of pictures of dresses. "I'm going to be in Daddy's wedding and have to pick the dresses. Auntie Marcie is, too. We like these ones so I'm taking them to show Gillian when she gets back. Are you going to be in the wedding?"

Marcie hadn't thought about that. She looked at him in horror.

Zack nodded thoughtfully. "I'm the best man."

"My daddy is the bestest man in the whole world," Jenny said.

"He is, but for the wedding, I'm called the best man. I hand him the ring so he can put it on Gillian's finger."

"Oh."

"Are you the maid of honor?" Zack asked Marcie.

Marcie smiled, knowing who the maid of honor would be. "Not me. Another friend of Gillian's. I'm a bridesmaid." At least she wouldn't be paired up with the best man! What would Zack think when he found out Gillian's maid of honor was the ninety-two-year-old friend of her great-grandmother?

"My bike's at the café," Jenny said, heading down the stairs.

"We'll swing by and pick it up," he said, making no effort to descend the stairs. "I still want to talk with you, Marcie," he said softly.

"You said enough on Sunday."

"We didn't talk at all."

She took a deep breath. "Since we're sure to run into each other if you stay around for a little while, I mean, in church and maybe bumping into each other on the street or something, or if Jenny comes to visit and you pick her up, though once Joe gets back, you won't have to do that anymore—and if you're going to be in the wedding, I guess we should make sure we know where we stand." She wanted to groan, she was babbling!

"I agree. And we want the wedding to go well."

"Well, you might take off again. The wedding is three months away," she couldn't resist saying. Then she was immediately ashamed of herself. The past was over. She needed to focus on the future and not contribute to the bad feelings between them. Every time there was a wedding in town, she was again reminded of all the planning they'd done, the bridesmaid dresses, the flowers, the music. Her dress, which still hung in the very back of her closet. She should have given it away years ago. It probably wouldn't even fit now. But it was the most beautiful wedding dress she'd ever seen. She couldn't bear to let it go, though it would probably never be worn.

Every wedding. She never spoke about it—not since her best friend's wedding when they'd discussed how hard it was for Marcie to be part of the wedding party. Surely the ache would fade in time. At least no one knew how sad weddings made her feel—no one but her and the Lord.

"I'm not taking off again," he said, a hint of impatience in his tone. "But that's the reason we need to clear things between us. So you'll understand and believe me."

She shrugged, knowing nothing he could say would change the past.

"Sally Anne's mother let me know she'd be happy to watch Jenny anytime. So why don't we go to dinner tomorrow?"

That was much too like a date. "How about lunch at the café instead?" At least she'd be on her own turf.

"Too public," he said.

"Dinner isn't public?"

"Not if we go to Portland. We'll have privacy in the city."

"I'd be more comfortable with lunch tomorrow." A romantic dinner in a Portland restaurant was more than she could bear. They weren't dating.

She needed to keep some distance, though it was growing harder every time she saw him.

"Pack a picnic, we'll eat at the marina," he countered.

She thought about it for a moment, then nodded. "Deal. I provide fantastic picnics, as it happens." A picnic could be equally romantic. Hadn't they stolen away as teenagers, picnicking on Carlisle beach, or in some of the woods around town? Being with Zack had been romantic in the old days. Could she keep her perspective meeting him for one last picnic?

"One o'clock? And I'll pay for the picnic—I invited you, after all."

"Okay, pick it up at one at the café. It'll have your name on it."

He turned and headed down the stairs. Marcie closed the door and leaned against it. She felt as if she'd run a mile. Excitement built as she thought about another picnic with Zack. This one wouldn't end in sweet kisses. Nor in the knowledge she'd see him again the next day and the day after. It would be a bittersweet lunch, memories of happier picnics crowding with the reality of the present. She sighed for what would never be repeated. It was just lunch, not a romantic tryst.

Zack turned into the driveway of his family home, hearing the bike slide a little in the back of the pickup truck. Jenny had been talking the entire trip from town, but he'd been only half listening. Tomorrow he'd have Marcie's undivided attention. He wanted to make sure she listened to him and understood that he regretted the past more than he could say.

Pulling in by the back door, he turned off the truck and gazed at the sea. The house sat on a bluff overlooking the Atlantic. It had been in the family for years. Currently his brother Joe and Jenny lived in it, but that would change when Joe married Gillian. He and Jenny were moving into the house Gillian inherited from her great-grandmother. She'd never had a place to call home, so Joe wanted her to have that house.

"Uncle Zack, can I call Sally Anne to tell her about the new dresses?" Jenny asked.

He smiled and nodded, then watched his niece dash into the house to call her best friend. He was grateful for this time at home. Chasing after a dream, he'd neglected family and friends. The fame and fortune he'd garnered wasn't as fulfilling as he'd thought it'd be. Traveling around Europe sounded glamorous—but the reality was it was racetracks he knew best, not capital cities. The telling moment, though, had been when Jacques had died.

He still couldn't believe his best friend for the past eight years was gone. He and Jacques had started out together on the team, bunked together until they earned enough in winnings to get their own rooms. Ate together when away from home. Shared parts of themselves no one else knew. They'd been closer than brothers. Zack had told him how often he thought about Marcie. Jacques had told him time and again to go back to see her. Zack never had. Now that Jacques wasn't around to tell him again, Zack had finally come home.

Shaking off the painful memory of his friend's fiery crash, he got out of the truck and lifted Jenny's bike from the back. Setting it near the back stoop, he glanced across the yard to the house next door. That's where Joe and Jenny would be moving—to Gillian's house—after the wedding. He looked at the family place. Maybe he could buy out Joe and put down roots.

Or, maybe, he thought as he shut the truck tailgate, life would be too uncomfortable in Rocky Point if Marcie didn't forgive him. Maybe he'd better make a fallback plan.

But he didn't want to. He wanted the future they'd once talked about. He'd learned from the past decade that going his own way had its rewards, but also drawbacks. Yet he was torn. The racing circuit was what he knew best. His life was exciting and predictable. For a moment he wondered if he was truly ready to stay in Rocky Point and give up the life in Europe. A lot to leave behind.

A lot to gain by staying in Maine. Only he could decide what he wanted. With plenty of time lately to consider everything, he'd discovered he wanted family, friends and love. They would last. The rest was fleeting. For a moment he frowned, wondering where he'd heard that before.

Marcie kept telling herself it was just a meeting to clear the air. She had no reason to feel anticipation or excitement. But as the morning wore on, her expectations rose. She tried not to remember meeting Zack for other picnics, but memories crowded in. Sometimes they'd meet on the lawn at the marina. Other times he'd drive them to the beach. Always together. This was so unlike other picnics, but she couldn't stop the hopeful feelings that grew. Would he tell her something that would ease the pain of the past? Give her insights into who he was today?

She'd ordered the lunch in his name and debated whether to be out front when he picked it up or walk over to the park early and be there when he arrived. If it was going to be awkward, better to be in the park and not have to walk over together. And the fewer people who saw them together, the less likely the rumor mill would spike.

"Marcie, your dad's out front," one of the busboys called when passing her office doorway.

She frowned. She hadn't expected her father to

drop by. As she walked from her office into the café, she realized she hadn't seen him at church on Sunday or at the picnic. That had flown from her mind when she had seen Zack at the picnic.

Bill Winter sat at a table by one of the large windows facing the street. He had a cup of coffee in front of him and was gazing out the window.

Marcie slid into a chair opposite him.

"Hi, Dad," she said. "If you'd told me you were here, I could have joined you."

He smiled at her. "You just did. Things going good?"

She nodded. He always asked that when they got together. "You missed the church picnic." Should she tell him about Zack?

"I also missed church Sunday. Too much going on."

"Like what?"

He looked at her a moment, then shook his head. "Fishing and things."

"Ah, the great excuse—you're closer to God fishing than anywhere else."

"Pretty much," he said.

Marcie shook her head when a waitress asked if she wanted anything. For some reason, today her father looked older than she'd noticed before. Her mother had died long ago and her father seemed content to live alone since Marcie had moved into her own apartment. She was his only child. She had wanted her own place several years ago, to be independent. But at what cost to her father? Had he regretted her decision? She'd fought against the idea of being an old maid caring for an aged father. Of course, before today she'd never thought of her dad as old. He looked all of his fifty-some years now.

Still, they remained close. Having dinner together most Sundays. Having lunch together now and then during the week. Sometimes she wondered if the Lord had plans for her to remain single all her days. She knew her dad would love grandchildren. No one in town had ever caught her eye since Zack left. And she didn't want to leave Rocky Point.

"So things are okay with you, Dad?" she asked again, fishing herself.

"Sure." He gave her a quick smile and took a sip of coffee.

Marcie wasn't convinced. Then it occurred to her he'd probably heard about Zack being back and was trying to find the best way to tell her.

"Dad, I know Zack Kincaid's back," she said softly, her eyes watching for his reaction. It would be hard not to in a small town like Rocky Point. Did her dad think to shelter her by never talking about Zack?

His expression hardened. "I haven't seen him, but I knew. You doing okay?"

She nodded. "He actually came to the picnic on

Sunday. He apologized for what happened all those years ago."

"No apology's enough," her father said gruffly, reaching out to pat her hand. "He hurt you badly, cupcake."

"I'm over that now," she said, relishing the comfort of her father's concern. He alone knew how much she'd grieved that lost love. He and the Lord.

"Stay strong. Stay focused on the Lord and He will see you through all the tough times."

She nodded, knowing it was true. "I'm fine." She smiled at her father. His love had always been as steadfast as God's.

"I might get some more fishing in this week," he said.

"If you catch enough, come over and I'll clean them and cook them for us."

"What's this *if?* Of course I'll catch enough."

Marcie laughed. "Of course—what was I thinking?" She tilted her head slightly. "How many did you catch on Sunday?"

He scowled. "Not enough for a meal."

She laughed again and pushed back from the table. "I've got to go, Dad. Let me know about the fish." She leaned over and kissed his cheek.

"You take care, cupcake," he said.

Something in his tone had Marcie pausing. "I will. You sure things are okay?"

"Right as rain."

Marcie bid him goodbye and went back to the office. Checking the clock, she realized it was later than she'd thought—and that much closer to time to meet Zack. She couldn't concentrate on anything. Might as well have stayed visiting with her father.

At five to one, she closed her office, telling Priscilla Cabot she was going to lunch, and left by the back door. The short walk to the marina did nothing to calm her nerves. She chose a picnic table in the shade with a view of the water and the boats bobbing on the gentle waves. The minutes ticked by. The breeze from the sea rustled the leaves of the oak shading the table. A sailboat moved silently on the horizon.

The café sack appeared in front of her on the table. She looked up. Zack took the bench opposite, his back to the water. "I thought you'd be at the café," he said.

She shrugged. "I came early."

He pushed the bag toward her. "Want to do the honors?"

Glad for something to do, she withdrew the lavish shrimp po-boy sandwiches, the small containers of coleslaw, along with utensils and napkins. The beverages were icy. Dessert was in another small container, which she rested on the collapsed bag.

Zack took the sandwich she offered, unwrapping it and taking a bite.

"Good," he said.

She nodded, feeling all thumbs. She unwrapped her own sandwich and nibbled on it. Her nerves churned. Now that they were face-to-face, with no hope of interruption, she wished she hadn't agreed to see him.

"I'm sorry," he said again, laying down the sandwich and gazing directly at her. "I handled it badly and I've regretted it ever since."

"It's been ten years. You couldn't call or write before now?" she asked, setting down her own sandwich. She opened the soda and took a sip, more for something to do than because she was thirsty.

He glanced away, then looked back. "I should have."

"Oh, Zack, apologies should never be made because they ought to be. They have to be sincere."

"I am sincere. I did it all wrong and hurt you and I'm forever sorry for that. It wasn't my intent."

"So what was your intent? We discussed marriage for months before deciding to do it. We knew we were young, but we thought we were ready. I thought we were ready. We planned the wedding all spring. Why not tell me you'd changed your mind?"

"I hadn't. Not exactly."

"Then exactly what?"

"I wanted to marry you, you know that. We talked about the wedding and not much about the future. You wanted a cottage by the sea. To stay in Rocky Point." He glanced away for a moment. "At first I thought I could be content working here, getting that house we talked about, settling down. Joe loved cars and I could have worked with him and done fine, I know."

"Sure." But he wouldn't have been happy. She knew that. His wildness was what had made him so irresistible. He had been restless, seeking a wider world than she had.

"Then, out of the blue, came a chance to drive on the race circuit. From Claude Moulet. I doubt you remember him, but he was someone my dad knew and had kept in touch after our folks died. Anyway, it was the chance of a lifetime. The only problem, I had to show up within two days to make the cut."

"So, scratch the wedding, forget the girl who was planning to share your life and take off. I see." As an explanation, it didn't help. She felt a rush of pain, remembering the heartbreak that had hit her so unexpectedly. That was the worst part—the lack of warning. She turned her face so he couldn't see the sadness she knew must be there. The remembered hurt was hard to hide.

He didn't reply for a moment. "I was eighteen. *You* were eighteen. We were kids. I got cold feet about getting married and was feeling stifled in Rocky Point. Our families have been here since the seventeen hundreds! I wanted to see something more than this spot of Maine. I was selfish and thoughtless and afraid I'd never get to see anything, do anything. And I knew I couldn't ask you to leave."

"I guess I should have picked up on that," she said slowly. Her heart hurt afresh with the thought of his getting cold feet, of regretting that he'd asked her to marry him. She had been so starry-eyed, thinking the world was perfect. Shame on her for not being more observant, more aware of his feelings. She blinked back tears. They had been kids, but as in love as she'd been, shouldn't she have seen what he was going through? She glanced at him; he was looking into the distance, regret clearly showing.

"I did all I could to squelch my fears. But they got bigger the closer to the wedding date we came. I didn't have a long-range career plan—what if we couldn't make it financially? What if there was nothing for me in Rocky Point, and you didn't want to leave? I knew that. I wanted to want what you wanted—that house near the sea, a white picket fence. How could I afford a house? What if we had kids? I didn't know anything about being a parent at eighteen. People were talking behind our backs about teenage marriages, the failure rate, the problems. The more I heard, the more I felt I couldn't make it. So when the offer came, it opened up the entire world. If I could make the grade, I'd have money to afford that house, I'd have security to offer you. So I left before I could be talked out of it." He drew in a deep breath and looked at her, shaking his head slowly. "I thought you could join me later. But by the time it was right, by the time I could afford it, I heard you'd bought the café and it sounded like you had things going your way. I knew you didn't want to leave Rocky Point. Buying the café anchored you even more. I did it all wrong," he said slowly. "I'm sorry, Marcie."

She stared at him for a long time, seeing the sincerity in his eyes. Her heart ached at the loss of the love they'd shared, at the dreams shattered. But life wasn't always fair. It didn't always go as she planned. Memories flitted through her mind—the church as it had been decorated with flowers and candles, the reception hall, the condolences of her bridesmaids, the beautiful white dress she'd never wear again. He'd gotten what he wanted and she'd grown happy enough over the years. She had her café and friends and a strong faith. God had truly blessed her. It was God's plan she sought.

"Thanks for the explanation," she said.

Silence grew. Marcie stared at the boats, began eating her sandwich. Zack studied her for a long moment.

"So what now?" he asked.

She looked at her sandwich, wishing she had

made them smaller. "We go on, I guess. What else is there?"

"I hope one day we might be friends," he said slowly. When she risked another glance, she could see the deep emotion in his eyes. She had not been the only one hurt by the past. Could she put it behind her? Could they one day be friends?

The pull of attraction she felt when around him suggested not. She'd forever yearn for more than friendship, for the love they'd once shared. She glanced around the marina. Everywhere she looked she saw bits and pieces of the past. They'd gone sailing several times over the summers in high school. She'd loved skimming the water while he handled the sails.

She shook her head to dislodge her thoughts. She did not want to dwell in the past.

Tears threatened. She'd loved him so much at one time and now all he wanted was to be friends. Swallowing hard, she nodded. "Sure, friends."

He reached out and took one of her hands in his.

She looked up into his dark eyes. Her heart skipped a beat. For a moment she wished she'd dare hold his hand and never let him go. Slowly she slipped her hand from his. "A lot's happened since then. I have a nice life and am content. You'll get tired of pokey old Rocky Point again and take off. You were right. I love it here and never wanted to live elsewhere. I have friends, my dad, a good business. I'm a homebody from the get-go."

"It's a good place to live. To raise a family. Joe's done well. We worked on cars together when we were teenagers. I'm thinking of asking him to let me buy in as a partner. I have enough knowledge to pull my own weight." He sat back a bit, as if deliberately placing distance between them.

"And how long before you miss the lights of Paris or the excitement of a race and you take off again?" she asked slowly. "This isn't your place anymore."

"It's my place, as much as it ever was. I'm back, probably for good." Now wasn't the time to go into his change of heart, his change of plans brought on by Jacques's death.

Marcie toyed with her sandwich, wondering how soon she could leave without looking like she was running away.

"How's your dad?" Zack asked.

"Fine. He's going fishing today."

"He always loved that. You go often?"

She shook her head. "I haven't been in a while. Too busy. But he's cut back his work hours to four days a week so he and his cronies can go as often as the weather permits."

"Did he ever get that boat he talked about?"

"No." She didn't want to talk about mundane things. She wanted to be alone, to think about what he'd said, try to see things from his point of view. *Please, Lord, give me insight to his feelings, so I can find forgiveness in my heart.*

Zack watched Marcie as she played with her food. She wasn't eating. The sandwiches were delicious, but he didn't have much appetite himself. He'd delayed speaking with her for the entire time he'd been back in town. Finally garnering courage to face her on Sunday and now today—and it seemed the wall she'd erected was stronger than ever. He wanted her forgiveness. He wanted her friendship. He wanted her laughter. Truth be told, he wanted her to love him again.

But her reaction to his apology had him fearing that would never happen. She hadn't said she understood his decision, that they had been kids but were older now and wiser. He felt wiser, with the experience of the last years. He was no longer the impetuous teenager longing for excitement and a lifestyle suited to only a few and panicking at the thought of being married. They could have had a baby that first year, which would have insured he could never leave. Things were different now. He was different. The thought of a baby, or two, did funny things inside. Would he be a good father? He'd do his best. If he could be half as good as his own father, it'd be okay.

"Have you heard from Joe and Gillian?" she asked politely.

He nodded, disappointed to think they were reduced to this—polite conversation about other people. Yet, what had he expected—that time would stand still until he chose to return? When, in fact, circumstances had dictated his return, not his choice.

"They finished sorting the things Gillian wants to bring here, cleaned the apartment and have started back. Gillian's driving her car, Joe the rented moving van. They expect to be home in a couple of weeks."

"How is it watching Jenny?"

He smiled. "I'm constantly surprised by what she says. I can't believe I let seven years of her life go by before getting to know her. She's awesome."

"She is. All the girls in her class are. I enjoy listening to them talk and am fascinated by how much they know and understand. I think as a kid I was a lot more oblivious to events going on around me. Of course, right now the main topic is the wedding. She's thrilled to be in it."

"I guess that's something most girls love," he said, daring a glance at her. He didn't want to talk about weddings, not so soon after explaining why he'd run from theirs.

Marcie looked at her watch. Did he see tears in her eyes? "I have to go." She gathered her sandwich and paper and stuffed it back into the bag. "Finish your lunch. Thanks for mine." She rose and headed back toward the café without a backward look.

I'm sorry, Marcie, he wanted to call out. *Please stay.*

Zack watched her leave knowing they were no closer at this moment than two days after he'd left her. But one thing was certain. After all this time, after all that had happened since he'd left, he still had strong feelings for Marcie Winter. She was skeptical, unbelieving in his commitment to stay in Rocky Point. So be it. He had a long way to go to regain her trust. His plans weren't firm yet, but they definitely included settling down and reconnecting with his family and old friends. If he were a praying man, he'd ask for help.

Another thing that had gone by the wayside when he'd left. It wasn't as if God was only in Rocky Point, Maine. But Zack didn't think He would have viewed his taking off in a good light. Probably had washed His hands of Zack years ago.

Could he mend fences there, as well?

Chapter Three

Zack finished the sandwich, trying to come up with an idea to prove to Marcie he could be trusted, that he knew his mind now and he was in it for the long haul. He hadn't a clue on how to convince her.

Seeing her again had planted the idea of the two of them together again. He wanted her back in his life and wanted to be a part of hers. He'd have to work at it, but one thing he knew for sure, she was worth it. She wasn't as receptive as he'd hoped. Yet perhaps that only showed him how much she'd once cared. Surely love that strong, a love they had thought would last their lifetime, wouldn't have faded completely away. Could he convince her to give him another chance?

"Zack," Sheriff Tate Johnson said, stopping by the table.

"Tate. Take a seat. You on patrol?"

Tate Johnson and Zack had gone to school together. Tate's parents ran the hardware store in the center of town. They'd shared more than growing up together. Both had been anxious to leave Rocky Point. Tate had gone to college in Boston, studying criminology. Ended up on the Boston PD for a couple of years. After his wife died, when his father had suffered a minor stroke, he'd returned to Rocky Point and was elected sheriff the next spring in a special election after old Sheriff Montgomery had died suddenly.

Maybe Zack should point out to Marcie that people did change their minds about Rocky Point. Tate was a perfect example.

"No patrol, just out walking around. In good weather it's the best way to keep in touch with everyone." He put a leg over the bench and straddled it. "In bad weather it shows everyone how devoted I am." He gave Zack a sardonic smile.

Zack laughed. "We all know you're devoted. Had to be to leave Boston to come here. This is not exactly the big city."

"Hey, it's home. Boston was fine. Got good training there. But things changed, stuff happened. Now I'm settled in Rocky Point."

"I don't suppose you are thinking of getting married again."

"Nope. Did that. I think the Lord has a different plan for me."

"Good luck," Zack said.

"You don't think so?"

"You might have an inside track at that." Zack did not want to talk about God or the plans He might have had once for Zack. "What do you know about a kid named Sean O'Connell?"

"Teenager. Gets in trouble sometimes, nothing major. Needs an outlet for some of that teenage energy. Why?"

Zack told him about meeting Sean at the picnic. "Any problem with driving too fast?"

"He doesn't have a car. Sometimes he borrows his mother's, but not often. Never heard of excess speed. So, he wants to race. You going to help him?"

"Maybe. Anywhere around to drive fast?"

Tate shook his head. "There was talk a few years back about a track in Portland, but nothing ever came of it. Liability insurance was prohibitive, I think."

"Any empty parking lots? Some of the driving techniques are more about controlling a car than speed. I could work with an obstacle course or something like that."

"There's a factory outside of Monkesville, not too far. Don't know who's in charge since they closed it down. Want me to find out?"

"If you could."

"You planning to stay around long?" Tate asked.

"Depends on a few things."

His old friend studied him for a moment, then guessed: "Marcie?"

"For one. Joe, for another. I want to see if he wants to go partners. He might like a bit more time off now that he's going to have a new wife."

"What about racing?"

Zack hesitated a moment, then said, "Racing's been every bit as exciting and fun as I thought it would be. Living in Europe, seeing different cities in different countries on a regular basis was thrilling in the beginning. Life seemed good...."

"But?" Tate narrowed his gaze as Zack trailed off.

"Five months ago my friend Jacques Burde was killed in a race. It was so unexpected. Jacques was daring but seemed to have a protective bubble around him. Until it popped. I've taken a long look at life since then. Touring Europe isn't as exciting as it once was. Between practice races and working with the mechanics to get the most out of the car, there isn't any time for sightseeing. I was on a treadmill from hotel to race course and back, then on to the next track."

"Sorry about your friend," Tate said.

He was quiet for a moment. It was hard to accept that Jacques wouldn't be celebrating victories again. Would never stay up late into the night discussing their different philosophies of life. Talking about a nebulous future where everything went their way.

"I guess every job had its routine aspects. Still an exciting profession. And you're at the top," Tate said.

"Being away from home wears on a person. The races are demanding. Every spare moment's needed to study the courses or work with the team for more performance from the car." He liked the money, the prestige and glamour. But most of the job was hard work and constant competition. Not to mention the edge of fear each race engendered. He'd done well. Since Jacques's death, however, he knew no one necessarily got out of racing alive. Time to retire while at the top.

"So you're going to be satisfied in Rocky Point?" Tate asked.

"I will. I'm not leaving. I'm enjoying getting to know my niece. It's almost a crime I waited seven years to meet her."

"Where does Sean fit in?"

"He asked for pointers. I'd like to see what's available. Maybe I could show a few others some aspects of racing. Emphasize the need for safety, the dangers of the sport. I wouldn't deny anyone the chance. Only, I'd advise more planning than I did. And to make sure the kid doesn't break someone's heart."

"Marcie's made a place for herself here. Don't go messing with that, Zack," Tate warned.

"My intentions are totally honorable."

The sheriff studied him for a moment. "You're going to try to win her back."

Zack nodded.

"An uphill battle. I don't envy you that task."

"Maybe impossible, but I need to try. I've missed her too much over the years to quietly sit on the sidelines. If there's any possible chance for us, I want it. I'm willing to do anything I can to have her forgive me and open her mind to the possibility of us as a couple again."

"Good luck." Tate rose. "I'll check on that parking lot for you. In the meantime, no racing on Ocean Side Drive."

Zack laughed. "None. My daring days are behind me."

"Somehow that's hard to believe." Tate touched the brim of his hat with a finger and resumed his walk.

At least his friend hadn't been outraged at his confession, nor too discouraging. Zack would have an uphill climb, but no matter what, he wanted Marcie in his life again.

Preferably as his wife.

Marcie walked into her office and shut the door. She sat at her desk, swiveled the chair around and gazed out the window at the back parking lot. Not the pretty view of Main Street the restaurant also afforded, but she wasn't seeing it anyway. A moment later she sighed softly and closed her eyes. *So, Lord, what's up with Zack? He wants forgiveness and I know I ought to give it. But it's hard. I was so hurt when he left. What should I do?* She waited several minutes and then opened her eyes as a knock sounded at the door. "I await your direction. Amen," she murmured quickly and turned.

"Come on in." Trying to look busy, she drew the schedule to the center of the desk.

"It's Trevor again," Jessica said without waiting a second. "He's driving me nuts."

"As in?" Marcie asked. She'd spoken to the teenager when Jessica first complained. She'd thought he understood.

"He thinks this is school and he can play hooky whenever he wants." She walked to the desk and leaned over, resting her palms on the flat surface. "Now he wants time off to go sailing with friends. Honestly, Marcie, you suggested I rotate the staff, and I've tried, but this kid is getting the best of me. And he has no drive or any kind of work ethic I can see."

"When does he want to go sailing?" Marcie asked, wondering if she made a mistake in hiring him.

"Today!"

"Send him in and I'll talk to him again and make it clear, work first or he can get a job somewhere else."

Jessica turned just as another waitress came to the door.

"Trevor took off," Ruth said. "Told me he told you he was going sailing."

Jessica turned back to look at Marcie.

"Okay, he's history. I'll call Marc and see if he can come in for the dinner shift. Can you two manage until then?"

Ruth looked at Jessica and nodded. "Piece of cake, boss," she said.

"I'll give you a hand in the meantime. This can wait," Marcie said, glancing at her desk. Physical activity would push out the niggling problem of Zack and his wanting them to be friends.

The afternoon passed swiftly, with business steady but not rushed. As the dinner hour approached, more and more customers arrived. Even with Marc's help, Marcie continued bussing tables, chatting with longtime customers and helping out a time or two with delivering orders to the tables. She loved her restaurant and was pleased so many of the town's residents seemed to, as well.

It was early evening when she took a break and ate standing in the kitchen. She had to get someone to replace Trevor. Helping out once in a while was not a problem, but that was not her job. Hers was to run the café, not clear tables. She'd ask Tim, her night manager, if he had any suggestions.

As she savored the salmon that seemed to melt in her mouth, she considered who was around who might want a job. Only a couple of high school students had applied for summer work. She'd hired both. The young woman had quickly learned, kept to herself and had never given a hint of trouble. She showed up a few minutes early every day and never left on the dot of nine. Too bad Trevor couldn't have been more like Sarabeth.

She'd ask around at church on Sunday to see if anyone knew a teen needing a summer job.

Standing in the bustling kitchen she watched as the sisters prepared the meals, the waitresses came and went with hot dishes and Oral washed dishes with a steady hand. He'd been with her from the beginning. People said he had a learning disability, but he'd learned to clean her dishes and utensils and did the job perfectly every day. His relief was an older woman, Martha Evenrode, who was retired but liked to keep her hand in, as she said. She talked a mile a minute, but was just as efficient as Oral. Why couldn't she have found summer workers with the same work ethic?

Once Tim arrived, Marcie filled him in on the situation and headed for home. She had neglected the work that waited on her desk, but wanted to leave. She felt drained from the day—starting with her meeting with Zack. What was she going to do about him? She needed to build immunity. Every time she'd seen him in the last few days, she'd felt confused, uncertain, giddy as a schoolgirl. That had to end. What they had was over years ago. He'd moved on, done what he wanted. And she had, too. She had all she needed, she thought as she let herself into her apartment.

Except a family of her own and grandchildren for her dad. Shaking off that thought, she rummaged in the fridge for the ice cream remaining from Jenny's visit. Time to indulge in chocolate! She'd take one day at a time, she vowed as she dished up the rich ice cream and drizzled chocolate on top. She wasn't sure if she was reading things as they were, or as she was beginning to wish they were. She had to decide—trust Zack or avoid him. Or was there a third option?

The next morning Marcie got to the café before seven. She wanted to get right to work and maybe have enough time later in the day to take a few hours off. She plunged in and it was two hours later before she noticed her morning waitresses giggling in the kitchen. She looked up and wondered what had them acting that way. Suzette straightened her pinafore and said something to April and then headed back to the dining room.

April stood at the door, peering after her.

Marcie's curiosity rose. "Is there a problem?" she asked, coming from her office.

April let the swinging door close and turned. "No problem, just the most gorgeous guy you ever saw. All summer visitors should look so good—we'd be even happier to serve them."

Marcie went to the door and looked out through the glass panel. In only a second she spotted Zack, with Suzette hovering over him.

"He's not a summer visitor. That's Joe Kincaid's brother."

"Wow, the race car driver?" April nudged her away and gazed out the narrow pane. "Now I see the family resemblance to Joe. Is he back for good?"

"I really don't know," Marcie said, walking away. That fluttery feeling was there again. Every time. She had to stop this. She poured herself a cup of coffee and considered things. Immunity wasn't coming easy. Maybe she needed to spend more time with him, have reality return. He was the same guy she'd once loved. On the phone last night with her best friend, Jody had said it was leftover feelings, nostalgia from the past. Was she right?

"I'll be out front," Marcie said, stepping around April and carrying her cup directly to Zack's table.

"Did you get his order?" she asked Suzette.

"Right here." She waved her order pad and smiled at Zack.

"You might want to give it to the cook." Sliding onto the chair opposite him, Marcie put her cup down and looked at Zack. Once Suzette had left, she asked, "What are you doing here and where's Jenny?"

"Jenny's at Sally Anne's for the day. Her mother's taking them to some store to look for new bathing suits. I gave her enough money to buy one and thanked Kimberly profusely for doing that. Otherwise, Jenny'd have to wait until her dad got home. I know nothing about bathing suits for seven-year-olds."

"That answers the first question, but why are you here?"

"Getting breakfast."

The amusement in his eyes told her he knew he was riling her up—and didn't care. For a moment she flashed back to high school and the times Zack had teased her. They'd ended up laughing in those days. Today, she was not amused.

"And you can't get food at home?" she asked sweetly, wishing he'd just get up and leave. Her senses seemed revved up. He looked fabulous. No wonder the waitresses were acting crazy. He'd had that effect on girls in high school. It seemed it carried forward with him.

"I'm not much of a cook. Didn't know you were, either," he said.

"I'm not. But I have the Cabot sisters. Remember they used to have that tea shop over near the courthouse? They retired, were bored and jumped at the chance to work at the restaurant when I asked them. I'm lucky to have them."

"They must be getting up in age," he said, studying her.

"Not really, barely in their sixties. I'll have them as long as they want to stay."

"So, this is a good choice for me to eat breakfast here."

He made it sound reasonable. But she knew better. "Don't you have something else to do?"

"I'm working at Joe's. Helping the guys with some of the cars. He's behind because of the burned hands." His brother had saved Gillian from getting burned when a fire was started at her house. He'd suffered burns on both hands, which had resulted in Zack's swift return home.

"We can make the meal to go," she offered, willing him to accept.

He laughed. "Or I can eat it here and have several cups of coffee to stretch out my time with you."

She frowned. "I'm not staying."

"So why come out?"

She looked around. "I try to greet customers

and keep an eye on things," she said, hoping he wouldn't guess her real reason.

"From a customer's point of view, much appreciated."

"Mmm." She took a sip of coffee, wishing now she'd never stepped out of her office.

"Morning, Marcie."

She looked up at Walter Pogral, a longtime friend of her father's.

"Hey, Walt, how are you?"

"Doing good. Your dad get his car fixed?"

"I didn't know anything was wrong with it," she said.

"Conked out on him in Portland last week. Called me to get him. Wondered how he got back to Portland to get the car when the shop there had it repaired. I haven't seen him all week."

"I saw him yesterday. He didn't mention anything about it."

"Guess he got another friend to take him back up to Portland." He looked at Zack.

"Aren't you Patrick and Molly's boy, the younger one, right? Zachariah?"

Zack nodded and stood to offer his hand. "I am."

"I thought you didn't live here, only Joe."

"I'm back."

"Ah, good. Sure have missed your dad all these

years. Well, I'll be heading for my table. Tell your dad I asked after him, Marcie."

"Sure will, Walt. Thanks for rescuing him." When the elderly man moved across the restaurant to sit at a small table next to the window, she looked at Zack as he sat back down.

"Wonder why Dad didn't call me," she murmured.

"Maybe he knew you'd be busy and Walt wasn't."

"I didn't even know he went to Portland last week," she mused.

"So? You two don't live in the same house anymore. Why would you?"

She looked at him. "It just seems strange, that's all. He never mentioned it." It felt odd to know she was not in the loop with her father's life. He hadn't mentioned it. As Zack said, why would he, necessarily? Still, she wished she knew more.

Suzette arrived with a heaping platter of scrambled eggs, sausage, hash browns and biscuits. "Here you go. Let me know if you need anything," she said with a flirtatious grin. She looked at Marcie. "Want anything?"

"No, thanks." She rose, the innocent questions lingering in her mind. What did she *really* want?

Zack watched her walk to the swinging door leading to the kitchen. He wished she'd stayed long enough to visit while he ate. The food was delicious. It was good to be back home where breakfast was what he was used to. Too many continental breakfasts to count.

Three more people stopped by to chat a few minutes. But he didn't see Marcie again before he left.

He headed for Joe's shop down near the docks and the cars that waited. The vintage automobiles were easy to work on, and a change from the turbocharged machines he'd been dealing with. These were basic engines, even simplistic. Get the engines running, repair the body and interior and the cars were good for another fifty to one hundred years. And with Joe's reputation, he earned top dollar.

"Hi, Mr. Kincaid."

Turning, Zack saw Sean O'Connell hurrying to catch up. The teen was dressed in the ubiquitous jeans and dark T-shirt, running shoes on his feet. His hair was nicely trimmed, and he looked eager. For a moment Zack saw a touch of hero worship reflected in Sean's eyes.

"Call me Zack," he said when the boy reached him. He began walking again.

"Thanks. I, uh, wondered if you thought about giving me pointers," the boy said, falling into step with Zack.

"Yeah. I asked around about a course or large parking area. Might be a possibility in Monkesville. Which means we could get some actual driving practice in, not just theory."

"Hey, that's cool." His face lit up in excitement, but an instant later he frowned, as if showing enthusiasm wasn't cool. "Is it true you're moving back here? I mean, I heard you raced all over Europe. This place has to be pretty quiet after that. There's nothing to do."

"It's home," Zack said, remembering feeling the same way when he'd been eighteen. Maturity changed his view. That and the experiences he'd racked up.

They reached the large warehouse that housed Joe's restoration business. The breeze blew from the sea, a ruffle of whitecaps in the distance. Inside a radio played, and the sound of men talking could be heard.

"Want to come in and look around?" Zack asked the teen.

The way his face lit up, Sean didn't need to answer, but did respond with an enthusiastic yes. "Maybe you can give me some pointers here," he said.

"Know your way around engines?"

"Not too much. I don't have a car and my mom won't let me mess with hers."

"I had mechanics working on my cars, but I always knew what they were talking about. A man needs to know all about the machine he's driving," Zack said.

As the morning wore on, Zack showed Sean the

cars that were being restored, showed him one of the engines and even let the kid do some of the work under supervision. Sean was delighted.

Zack recalled the hours and hours he and his brother had spent during the long summer days when they were teens, first too young to drive, then older and able to drive the cars they worked on. Nothing more enjoyable than hanging over a dirty engine and getting it to purr.

He glanced at Sean, filthy up to his elbows, a smear of dirty oil on his cheek. But the concentration was admirable. The kid picked up things quickly.

"Your mother know where you are?" Zack asked. He shook his head in disbelief. Watching Jenny was changing him. He would never have asked that a month ago.

Sean looked up. "Not exactly. She knows I hang out around town. She's at work, she won't worry."

"Give her a call. We'll take a break and grab a bit of lunch—it's after one."

Sean hesitated a moment and then shook his head. "I can take off."

"After lunch." Zack pulled back and went to clean up, calling over his shoulder, "My treat."

Naturally he headed back to Marcie's café. Maybe one part of his plan should include a daily meal at her restaurant. The food was good and he could always hope the owner would come out to check on the customers while he was there.

The café was about half-full when they entered. They were seated and their orders taken. Zack recommended the shrimp po-boy, but Sean opted for the mushroom burger with fries. They both had iced tea to drink. Zack looked around while they waited for their order to be filled.

He was surprised a minute later to see Marcie come from the kitchen with a large plastic tub on her hip. She began clearing a table across the room. As if she could feel his stare she looked up. For a moment he wasn't sure if he saw a welcome in her gaze or not, but she looked away and continued her task.

When the waitress brought their orders, he asked if Marcie had a minute.

"She's working, but I'll ask." It wasn't the woman from that morning. This one was older and definitely not in a flirtatious mood.

"You're taking the support-your-local-business bit too seriously," Marcie said a minute later. She had the plastic tub on her hip, empty now.

"Good food. What's not to like?" he asked. After introducing Sean, he asked, "What are you doing?"

"I'm shorthanded. I had to fire one of my summer hires—too lazy. Until I find someone else, I'm filling in."

Zack scrambled around for something else to say so she wouldn't leave. "I thought I'd offer to look at your dad's car if you like. I know he got it fixed in Portland, but I could give it a checkup, make sure it's in tip-top condition."

She studied him thoughtfully. "Now, why would a big fancy race car driver want to do that?"

He shrugged. "Just to be neighborly and all. Seeing as how I'm moving back."

She flicked a glance at Sean then looked back at Zack, a gleam in her eye. "Go for it."

He didn't trust that gleam. Memories of days when she'd been up to something surfaced instantly. He remembered some of the ideas she'd had when they'd been kids. TP-ing the mayor's big elm tree before the elections one year, or their Senior Sneak day, and the hijinks they'd devised. "What does that mean?" he asked warily.

"Nothing. I'm sure he'd appreciate the offer." She turned and headed to another table recently vacated. Glancing over her shoulder she shook her head. *Not!*

Zack took another bite of his sandwich wondering if offering to help her father would gain him any brownie points with the woman. But he didn't trust that gleam.

"What was that about?" Sean asked.

"Her father's car died on him in Portland. It was repaired but I thought I'd check it out."

Sean looked at Marcie. "Do you think she'd hire me to clear tables?"

"I have no idea. Do you have any experience?"

"My mom makes me clear my place every night." Zack hid a smile and nodded. "Go for it."

The kid took a huge bite of his burger, then a deep breath as he approached Marcie. Zack watched as the two of them talked for a while.

Sean almost floated back to the table. "She said she'd give me a try," he said, taking his seat again. "Man, that would be so cool if I could make some money this summer. It's tight at my house, you know?"

"I know how that can go," Zack said, remembering how his father made him earn any money needed to work on the cars. It didn't hurt kids to learn the value of a dollar early.

"As soon as I finish lunch, I can start work. I need to call my mom. She'll worry if I'm not home when she gets home, but Marcie said the job goes till nine."

"You can hang out around the garage some, too, if you'd like," Zack said.

"You mean it? I could? That's awesome. The job here is from noon to nine, with an hour for a dinner break. I could come mornings. Man, that's so awesome."

When they finished eating, Sean went to the back to begin the new job. On impulse Zack headed for the insurance agency that Marcie's dad owned. It was on a cross street, not too far from the town square. The good thing about Rocky Point was nothing was very far from the town square.

He entered the one-story brick building and noticed the coolness after the afternoon sun. The lobby was empty except for a receptionist at the desk.

"May I help you?" A woman looked up from typing at the reception desk.

"Bill Winter available?"

"Zack Kincaid? Well, I never thought I'd see you back in Rocky Point. I'm Betty Thompson. It's been a while since anyone's seen you."

"It has. Nice to see you again."

She looked at him a moment, then reached for the phone.

"Someone here to see you," she said. She listened and then replaced the receiver. "Go on in."

Zack thought he heard her say *and good luck* under her breath, but he wasn't sure.

Opening the door, he was startled when he saw Marcie's father. The once-robust man looked decades older. His hair had receded and gone completely white. He was thinner than Zack remembered and had a sallow complexion.

Bill stood offering his hand, then let it drop when he realized it was Zack. "Get out of here. You have your nerve, coming back. Didn't you wreak enough havoc before? Stay away from my daughter!"

Conscious of Betty in the reception area, Zack closed the door behind him.

"I've apologized to Marcie and I apologize to you. What I did was wrong." He wasn't going into details with Bill. If Marcie forgave him, it would be enough.

The man sat in his chair, picked up a paper and pretended to read it. "Shut the door on your way out," he said.

"I heard you had car trouble in Portland. I came to offer to look at it for you."

Bill snapped his head up at that. "Where'd you hear such a thing?"

"Walt told us this morning."

"Us?"

"I was eating breakfast at Marcie's. She was sitting with me." He knew saying it that way made it sound better than the reality. But he wanted the old man to cut him some slack.

"Marcie knows?"

That surprised Zack. "Was it a secret?"

"No! Of course not. Why would it be?"

"She didn't know you were going to Portland."

"No reason she should. The car's fine. I don't need you looking at anything of mine. Get out of here."

Zack nodded once. "I'll be going. But if you change your mind, let me know. I'm staying at Joe's."

Now he knew why Marcie had suggested he offer his help. She knew the reception he'd get. For a moment he felt a pang for the way things had turned out. In the past he'd been as welcome at the Winters' home as he had been in his own. It was more than Marcie he'd hurt, obviously. Could he make amends here, too?

Chapter Four

Marcie's apartment seemed especially empty when she entered shortly before seven that night. She opened the windows to let the evening breeze blow through. She'd eaten at the café, and was not going to make a habit of ice cream every night. But after the bustle of the café, her quiet place seemed lonely.

The phone rang. Maud Stevens was on the other end.

"Have you heard from Gillian?" Maud asked. The older woman was going to be Gillian's matron of honor. Maud had been best friends with Gillian's great-grandmother—the two had gone to school together and remained friends until Sophie's death earlier that year.

"Not directly, but Jenny talks to her almost every night. She and Joe finished closing down Gillian's apartment and are on their way back."

"Gillian mentioned you and Jenny were picking

out bridesmaid dresses. I do hope you two remember my age. I can't be wearing some low-décolletage dress."

"No, ma'am, we have no low-cut dresses. The age range for this wedding party is seven to ninety-three. We have to accommodate all of us."

"Well, good. And no green. I look sick as a dog if I ever wear green."

Marcie smiled. "I'm sure once Gillian decides, she'll have us all over her at her house to see, and we can veto anything we hate."

"She is such a dear. I just wish Sophie had met her."

Marcie heard her sigh. "At least Gillian knows a lot about her great-grandmother because of the stories you're telling her."

"There's that. I heard through the grapevine that rascal Zack Kincaid has come back. Is he staying for the wedding?"

"Actually, I believe he's to be the best man."

The silence on the other end caused Marcie to smile again. She couldn't wait until Zack saw who he would be paired with.

"Well, that does beat all. Does he know I'm matron of honor?"

"I don't believe he does, unless Jenny's told him. It should be interesting, don't you think?"

"He was wild as a boy. But good, too, you know that."

"Except when running out on a wedding with

scarcely any notice," Marcie said dryly. She remembered him as exciting and wild and so much fun she lived for the time they spent together.

"I'm sure he had his reasons. Do call and tell me if Gillian calls."

"I will, Maud. You take care."

Marcie had been to several weddings over the years as different classmates had married. The first had been the hardest, when Shirley Norris married Bruce Hartwell. It had been almost a year to the day after her own had been scheduled. She had declined all offers to be a bridesmaid until her best friend Jody had married five years ago. She couldn't hold off against her friend's blandishments.

It was hard now that Zack was back to ignore the memories of her excitement at getting married, the planning and work that had gone into the wedding. How her dad had sent all the reception food to a soup kitchen in Portland so it wouldn't go to waste after the event had been so unexpectedly canceled.

Sinking on her sofa, she leaned her head back. *Lord, I'm praying for some wisdom here. What should I do about Zack? Forgive and move on? Try to be friends? I thought I had gotten over the pain of his leaving, but that ache is in my heart. Lord, I need You more than ever. Speak to me, I pray. Give me Your guidance and love.*

Marcie remained on the sofa for several minutes,

then rose and went to get her Bible. She'd read where it opened and hoped the Lord was telling her what to do.

The Bible fell open to Isaiah and she read, *Behold, I have graven thee upon the palms of my hands.* That verse didn't just apply to her. It applied to all God's children, including Zack. She didn't agree with how Zack had backed out of their marriage, but God still loved them both. It was up to her to find forgiveness in her heart for him. It didn't mean she had to put herself in a similar situation again. She didn't have to plan a life with Zack, just forgive the mistake of the past and draw closer to the Lord.

Zack and Jenny stood on the edge of the bluff overlooking the tiny beach below. The setting sun was behind them, the sky darker on the horizon before them. The sea was growing gray and dark.

"When it gets warmer, Daddy will take me down to the beach to play in the water. I can't swim too good yet, though sometimes Melissa and Sally Anne and I go to the pool at the high school. When Sally Anne's mom can take us."

"Don't go down to the beach alone," Zack said, echoing what his parents had drummed into his head. He hadn't thought about them in a long while. It was hard to believe they'd been gone so long. He missed them still. Probably always would.

"I won't. Did you and Daddy play there when you were little boys?"

"Oh, yeah, and our folks made sure we always had a grown-up with us." He felt an awesome responsibility for this little girl while her dad was gone. It made him feel more connected to his parents—sharing the same admonitions they'd given. Watching the future generation of Kincaids grow. Would he and Marcie have had kids? By now they could have had a houseful.

Jenny looked out to the horizon. The sun slipped away and before long it would be dark. There were lights on in the house behind them to guide them back.

"Over there is Europe," she said, pointing east.

"Right you are."

"My daddy and I came out here a lot to pray for you."

That surprised Zack. "Well, thank you."

"Daddy prayed you would find your way home. Were you lost, Uncle Zack?"

"Maybe a bit," he said.

"And we prayed you'd always be safe. And God kept you safe and helped you find your way back home." She sounded pleased with her conclusion.

Zack wondered if God had listened to his brother's prayers and kept him safe. His friend Jacques could have used some prayers. Maybe he wouldn't have died in that crash. Zack rubbed his hand over his face, wishing he could erase the memory of the fiery collision, the sick certainty the instant he knew that his friend was dead.

"Did you pray for us?" Jenny asked, looking up at him. "We aren't lost but we always need God."

The shrill ring of the old phone in the house echoed in the night air.

"I bet that's Daddy," Jenny said, turning to run to the house. Zack followed, glad he hadn't had to answer that innocent question. He should have been praying all along, but after leaving like he had, he hadn't felt worthy. He still didn't. God didn't want people to hurt those they love. Or to turn away from Him. Yet Zack had done that and more.

Could he come back and fit in? Or would his restless spirit keep him from the contentment his brother seemed to have found?

Some of that was due to Gillian, he knew. The Lord wanted man to have a helpmeet and Joe had Gillian.

He'd had a good one himself and carelessly thrown it all away.

Jenny was talking a mile a minute when he stepped into the kitchen. She regaled whoever was on the phone with her day at Sally Anne's, the new swimsuit she'd bought with money from Uncle Zack and the plans for swimming later in the week if the weather stayed warm.

"When are you going to be home?" she asked.

She nodded and looked at Zack. "Okay. Here's Uncle Zack. They'll be home next week," she said, handing him the phone and scampering out of the room.

"Hello?"

"It's Joe. We're in Saint Louis. Saw the arch today. I told Jenny we stopped at an internet café and sent some pictures, so she can see them. How are things going?"

"Good. Kimberly helped today, taking Jenny. I hope she doesn't expect me to reciprocate. Two giggling seven-year-olds would be more than I can cope with." He leaned back in the chair remembering trying to keep up with her energy. And the cute things she unexpectedly said during the course of a day.

Joe laughed. "She won't. I'm sure she's glad to have Jenny with Sally Anne. Together they entertain themselves. How was the church picnic?"

"Fine." He went on the alert. He didn't want to discuss his meetings with Marcie, not yet.

Joe waited a couple of seconds. "Marcie there?"

"Yeah. We talked. I apologized. And saw her father today to apologize. He's aged." Zack carefully kept his tone neutral.

"Haven't we all?"

"A teenager I met at the picnic wants to learn more about cars, so I had him at the shop today.

He might stop by again. He's smart, and won't be unsupervised."

"Your call. If you're serious about going in partners, we'll talk more about it when I get back. Which should be mid to late next week. We're heading for Chicago next, then New York and Boston. Gillian hasn't seen anything farther east than Vegas, so we're both enjoying it. Just wish we could drive together."

"Should have gotten a huge moving van and put her car in it."

"Yeah, right. Take care of my daughter."

Zack smiled. "Always. You two enjoy the sightseeing." He hung up slowly, thinking about what Jenny had said on the bluff.

"God, if You're still listening for me," he said. "I'd, uh, like to ask Your blessing on my brother and his fiancée as they drive across the country. Please keep them safe," he added, feeling awkward. He waited a heartbeat then went to show Jenny the photos Joe had emailed.

When he tucked her into bed later, he went back to the computer to look again at the pictures. A lot were singles, either of him or Gillian. She was lovely with her tawny golden-blond hair and bright blue eyes. So different from Pamela, Joe's first wife. In addition to being beautiful on the outside, she was as beautiful on the inside. Sweet and loving to Joe and Jenny, and welcoming to him.

Of course, they had no past together.

He gave in to the desire to hear Marcie's voice once again. He dialed her number, knowing he had the perfect excuse and hoping she wouldn't hang up on him.

"Hello?"

The sweet sound warmed his heart. "Hi, Marcie, it's Zack."

"Now what?"

He settled in the chair, taking it as a good sign that she hadn't hung up on him.

"Joe sent some pictures, thought you might want to see them."

"How?"

"I could forward them to your computer. Or, you could come over here and see them on his. He sent them to Jenny tonight." He hoped she'd choose to come over. It was a short drive from town and not that late.

"Go ahead and forward them."

"Okay, hold on so I can make sure they go through." Disappointment flared. Still, he had her on the phone. He sent the pictures and picked up the phone again.

"Did you get them?"

"I'm still waiting for my computer to power up."

"How's Sean working out?" He was getting desperate to keep her on the phone. He wanted to find out what she was doing. See if he could detect any softening toward him.

"It's only been one afternoon, but so far, so good. He's only sixteen, but seems to have a much better work ethic than the kid I had before. I have another high school worker, Sarabeth. She's shy as all get-out, but does a good job. Wait, the photos are here. Oh, look at the arch. I've never been to Saint Louis. Wow, the river is not as blue as I thought it'd be."

Zack had never been to the Mississippi, either. He'd seen many of the countries in Europe but had never toured his own. Was that something Marcie would like to do someday?

"Thanks for sending the pictures," she said.

"I saw your dad today," he said, hoping to forestall her ending the call.

"I bet he did not take to your idea of looking at his car," she said with a trace of humor in her tone.

"Not at all. Told me to get out and stay away from you." He wanted to ask if that was her wish as well, but dared not. As long as she never told him flat out to stay away, he felt he had a chance. "Marcie, he looks far older than I remember."

"It has been ten years."

"Is he okay?"

"Sure, why wouldn't he be?"

Zack didn't want to put ideas into her head, but to him the man looked so different it was startling.

Marcie saw him every day, so it wouldn't be as apparent. But Marcie was his only child. If there was anything wrong, Bill would certainly let her know.

"Forget it. I just wondered."

"We all get old," she said. "Speaking of which, have you met the rest of the wedding party?"

"No, why?"

"I think Gillian plans to have a small dinner party when they get home, so everyone can meet the others. I know everyone, but I'm not sure you do."

"No problem, it's not like I have a lot going on right now," Zack said.

"Sorry Rocky Point doesn't offer the excitement of London or Rome."

"That's not what I meant and you know it. I need to get my own place, firm up the partnership with Joe and wind up things in Europe. Right now I'm just a babysitter for Jenny."

"I've got to go. Thanks for sending the pictures."

He hung up, wishing he'd never made that comment. It reminded her of his leaving and he was trying to get her to think more about his staying.

"Zack Kincaid's in the restaurant," April said, passing the door to Marcie's office the next morning.

Despite the skip of her heart, Marcie kept her

head down, eyes focused on the list of dishes she was preparing for the upcoming weekend. "I'm busy. See he gets what he wants like everyone else," she said.

For a moment she couldn't concentrate. They'd talked for a while last night on the phone, almost as when they were teens. Back then he'd drop her at home and then call her as soon as he got home. Her father used to ask what they'd have to talk about since they'd just seen each other. That had never been a problem in the past.

His comment at the end still bothered her. There was little to do in Rocky Point for a person used to large cities and cosmopolitan entertainment. Her own life revolved around her business, church and her friends. And during the week because of the long hours she put in, she didn't socialize much. Still, she liked her life. She didn't yearn for anything else—unless it was a family of her own. She liked children. Would love to give her father some grandkids.

Sometimes she felt a touch of envy for those friends who had loving husbands and rambunctious children.

She shook her head, trying to dislodge those thoughts. The Lord would provide her a partner in His own good time. If that was His will. Some women never married. She hoped she wasn't one.

She really did want children. And her dad would love a grandson to teach to fish!

It was just after nine when she gathered a folder and her purse. She was going to give a new lobster distributor in Portland a chance to work with her and had scheduled an interview at their offices later this morning.

The road to Portland wound through the forest with glimpses of the sea from time to time. She had chosen the highway for the scenic views rather than the speed the interstate would have given her. She was in no particular hurry and relished this time to herself. Her manager was in charge at the restaurant and could handle any emergency. It was almost like a holiday.

The meeting went well and once finished, Marcie decided to eat lunch at one of the restaurants in the Old Port section of Portland. The meal was delightful and she wondered if the Cabot sisters could add another entrée to the menu.

It was early afternoon when she headed back. Once the traffic from Portland thinned, she sped up a bit. Passing one car, she looked in her rearview mirror in surprise. It was her father. He was going the same way she was—away from Portland and toward Rocky Point.

Had he been in Portland again? Why?

Another car passed her father and came in behind her. She considered the idea of slowing down and then letting her father pass her so she could follow him home. But before she could act on that, he turned off. Puzzled, Marcie continued home. She'd call her dad later to see what was going on.

But, though she tried every half hour all evening long, her father didn't answer. Finally after nine, really concerned, she drove over to her childhood home to check on him. It was dark. His car was not in the carport. Where was he?

She parked and wrote a short note asking him to call her when he got home, then opened the front door and put it prominently on the table where he kept his car keys. He must have made plans that she didn't know about. Not that she should. When she'd moved from home, she'd wanted her own privacy and her dad was entitled to his.

The next morning just before the lunch rush began, her father called.

"Went fishing with some friends," he said.

"I saw you on the highway yesterday and then you turned off. You were coming from Portland," she said.

"I missed the turn going up, had to turn around and go back down. Didn't catch anything, either."

She smiled at the disgruntled tone. "Can't catch something every time. I just wondered since I couldn't reach you at home last night."

"A man should not have his daughter watching him every moment."

Marcie laughed. "Like it's every moment. If I hadn't seen you on the highway near Portland I would never have known. I was surprised to see you, that's all."

"What were you doing in Portland?" he asked. "I didn't know you were going up."

Marcie explained. They chatted a few minutes, then hung up. She needed to see more of her father. Maybe they could have lunch together after church Sunday. He rarely missed church services. She was worried about him. He was all the family she had. Time to get to the bottom of whatever was going on.

Sunday Marcie dressed in a light blue suit, growing more nervous as the time for church approached. She gazed at her reflection in the mirror. "I can do all things through you, Lord," she told herself. "Even meeting Zack again in front of everyone at church. Each time I see him, it will become easier." If he even showed up. So far since he'd returned, he had not attended church. Trinity was her church—and the place they were to have exchanged vows ten years ago. Many members of the congregation had been invited to the wedding. She knew they would be remembering. As she would yet again. For the past few years, except for attending other weddings, she'd been able to push away the memory of her own special day. Now that Zack was back, it came to the forefront every time she entered the church.

Turning, she didn't feel her pep talk had soothed that much, but it was the best she could do. Gathering her purse and Bible, she headed out. She and her father usually sat together in church, neither having a partner in life's journey.

Puffy clouds doted the expansive blue sky as she walked the few blocks to the church. Parking was never a problem in the church lot, but whenever the weather was nice, she preferred to walk. The breeze from the sea held the tang of salt she loved. Today felt fresh and clean. "Today is the day the Lord has made, I will rejoice and be glad in it," she recited as she approached the white clapboard church with its traditional steeple. She recognized everyone she saw, greeting those close enough.

Her father stood near the double doors, watching for her. He smiled when he saw her. He did look older. And thinner. Was there something wrong, or was it a reality check? He was no longer a young man.

"Good morning, cupcake. You look fresh and happy."

"It's a beautiful day. Not fishing today?"

He shook his head. "Want to take my best girl out for lunch."

"We could drive down to Kennebecport," she suggested.

"Sounds good. See you after Bible study."

Marcie almost held her breath when she entered the church sanctuary later. She had not seen a sign of Zack or Jenny. Maybe he had not brought the little girl after all, though Jenny loved Sunday school. If Zack didn't bring her, maybe Marcie could offer for next week. No, Joe and Gillian would be back by then. They never missed.

But Zack often had. Maybe he *was* the same Zack Kincaid, after all, she thought with a sigh of relief, tinged with disappointment.

Zack and Jenny entered the back of the sanctuary. The place was almost full. Thankfully, he found an empty spot in the next to the last row and ushered Jenny in. He had only wanted to drop her off at church with a promise to pick her up afterward. But she'd insisted they attend together.

"We always sit up front with Aunt Marcie," she said, scooting in and looking around.

"This is fine," he said, sitting on the wooden pew. Glancing around, he noticed several people looking at him. He nodded and looked forward.

The man next to Jenny offered a hand to Zack. "Welcome to Trinity Church. We're glad you could join us. I'm Samuel Bowmont."

"Zack Kincaid." He shook hands, and then nodded to the man's wife when she was introduced. At least these people didn't seem to know him or the episode that might have played out in this church.

The organist began and the chatter quieted. Zack stared straight ahead. If he didn't make eye contact with anyone, no one would speak to him. He was uncomfortable surrounded by so many people he'd known most of his life, but on whom he'd turned his back for so long. Jenny reached for a hymnal and began turning the pages. He remembered days gone by when his parents had brought Joe and him to church. And later, when he and Marcie were dating in high school, they'd sat together. He'd loved singing the different hymns. Singing had been the best part of the service when he'd been younger.

His gaze found Marcie. She was sitting next to her dad near the front. His throat tightened as he gazed at the back of her head. So many memories and regrets.

The music changed slightly and people rose to their feet. He stood and stared at the hymnal Jenny shared with him. She already had the correct page number.

Feeling awkward after having shunned church for so many years, nevertheless he began singing the familiar hymn. The words remembered, the melody returned.

It felt odd to be in the church he'd grown up in. He couldn't help thinking about the day he was supposed to marry Marcie. The church had been decorated with flowers, white roses and some small white flower and lots of green. They'd had the rehearsal, Zack's fear building. Then the fateful call had come earlier that week. He'd wrestled with his decision for days, finally deciding the night before to take the opportunity Claude had offered.

He'd known it was wrong to leave like that. But he couldn't stay. The lure of a racing future had proved too strong. The opportunity had been amazing. Who else would have been called from obscurity to be given a chance to make a name for himself in the racing world?

Now he wondered how she'd managed to come into this church Sunday after Sunday, remembering how they'd decorated it. Did she attend other weddings? Did she always remember?

How could she not?

Joe and Gillian would be married here in September. Once again the old building would be decorated for a beautiful bride. Vows would be exchanged. Happiness was never guaranteed, but he had a feeling it would permeate his brother's marriage.

Look at him. He'd taken the opportunity of a lifetime and for years had been consumed with the racing, the fame, the money. Yet it all seemed shallow and unimportant when faced with dying young like his friend. No wife mourned Jacques. No children carried on the family name. Only his parents and friends remained to keep the memory of his life alive.

Lay not up for yourselves treasures on earth. The old verse popped into mind. He'd done just that. So had Jacques. What good had it done either of them?

The service seemed interminable. He was uncomfortable with his thoughts. He glanced at his watch a half-dozen times. Minutes had never moved so slowly. Finally—the last hymn.

When the music ended, he took Jenny's hand and hurried her from the pew and out the double doors.

"Where are we going?" she asked, clutching her Bible and almost running to keep up with his longer stride.

"Home. We'll barbecue and maybe go down to the beach."

"Yippee. I haven't been so far this year."

"I know, you've said it a dozen times a day since Memorial Day."

"That's when summer starts and Daddy says we can only go swimming in summer."

He smiled at her. "And then only if it's warm enough. Which it is not today. But we can walk along the shore in the cove."

They were in the truck and heading out of the parking lot when he spotted Marcie and her dad walking toward Bill's car. She recognized Zack's truck and waved—probably at Jenny. Bill Winter glared at him, his anger almost palpable through the windshield. He wasn't accepting Zack's apology even if Zack could get Marcie to do so.

He refused to become discouraged. He knew what he wanted now and sooner or later would figure out a way to get it.

In the meantime, he would enjoy his time with his niece.

"How about we stop and pick up a picnic lunch and have that on the beach?" he asked.

"Okay!" Jenny's enthusiastic response made him smile. Too bad there wasn't someone else with them to share the moment.

That afternoon Zack sat in a growing patch of shade watching Jenny play along the water's edge. He and his brother had spent many hours at the beach with his parents when they were younger, and then just the two of them when they were deemed old enough to stay safe. He and Marcie had also shared the beach when they were in high school. The days had been fun, swimming in the cold water, warming up in the sun, talking about their future. Carefree and happy, just as childhood should be.

He'd been to the beach in Cannes, on the Costa Blanca in Spain and along the Italian Riviera. The Med was definitely warmer. But here, surrounded by the rocky bluffs behind him, the small sandy spot was home.

"Can we walk again, Uncle Zack?" Jenny asked, running over to him. She'd made a basic sand castle and left it to the incoming tide that would sweep it away.

"We can." He made sure the remnants of the picnic were stowed safely above the high-water mark and took her hand to walk along the water. They had taken off their shoes and splashed in the cold Atlantic. He wondered if he was too old to enjoy swimming later in the summer. The water hadn't seemed as cold when he was a child.

"Tell me about you and daddy playing here," she said.

Zack had discovered soon after he had returned to Rocky Point that Jenny loved hearing any stories he had to tell about her father when he was little. It gave Zack an odd sense of continuity. One generation passing on stories to the next. Would his own children like to hear about his life when he was a child?

Would he have children one day or was he destined to go it alone?

The beach was entirely in shade by the time they decided to return to the house on the bluff above them. Zack carried the sack that held the trash from lunch, while Jenny carried her shoes and ran up the wooden steps. When he reached the top she was halfway to the house.

She turned and yelled, "The phone's ringing," and then resumed her race to the house. Zack followed quickly. It was early yet for Joe and Gillian to be calling. But it was Sunday—maybe they'd decided to stop early for the day. He couldn't imagine anyone else calling.

"It's for you, Uncle Zack," Jenny said when he entered the kitchen. The phone receiver had been laid on the counter.

"Thanks, Jenny. Go rinse off the sand and salt water," he said, putting down the bag and reaching for the phone. "Kincaid," he said.

"Hey, Zack, Thomas Sterling here. How's it going, guy?" Thomas was the team leader and chief liaison with their major sponsor.

Zack almost groaned when he heard Thomas on the line. He was trying to put that part of his life behind him. "I'm doing well, how're things with you?"

"Not so good, Zack. We need you back. How's your brother?"

"I told you before, I'm bowing out. I'm needed here." He'd met opposition, but he'd been clear he was pulling out of racing. Joe's burned hands were the perfect excuse to break away, and he had no desire to return.

"Hey, man, we can hire help for your brother.

So far we haven't found a replacement behind the wheel for you! We haven't even finished in the money since you left."

Zack leaned against the counter. It might be a long call. "I'm dropping out, Thomas, you know that."

"Hey, man, you know that Jacques's death hit everyone hard. But it was a fluke, a freak accident. You've been racing ten years, you've never even come close to buying it. We need you, man. Tell me what it'll take to get you back. A bigger percentage? Different machine? What? The end of the circuit's around the corner. You're needed, buddy. Here, not in some forgotten corner of Maine."

"It's not a question of money or car. I'm done. That's all."

"It's not, Zack. I need you, man. The team needs you, man. And your contract states you'll be here."

No racer did the job solo. There were sponsors, pit crews, publicity people, managers. Quite a few people made their livelihoods supporting a racing team. And his team was the best. But there were two other drivers for the team, and a slot now for a newcomer.

"Stockholm's coming up, Zack. You know you always ace that course. No one has come close to your last record there. Tell you what, I'll see about upping the percentage of the take if you race that one course. Just Stockholm, man. You can do it in your sleep. Say you'll do it, then we'll talk again."

Zack wavered. Stockholm was a tough course. He'd been the winner three years running, last time by a healthy margin. For a moment he thought about Jacques. His friend had challenged him before that last race to meet in Stockholm to see who was the faster. Would Jacques have raced the course if Zack had been killed?

"I'll think about it," he said. Obligations, responsibilities, duty—all had been instilled in him by his parents. Did he have the right now to throw others under the bus so he could get what he wanted?

"Great. You'll need to be here in a couple of weeks. The latest car tests show the engine on the T is superefficient and the torque ratio is amazing. It's the fastest machine we've ever had. You need to get familiar with it. I'll send the tickets."

"Hold on. I said I'd think about it, not that it's a done deal." The dilemma was ironic. Leave them in the lurch as he had Marcie, or stand by his word as he had not done with her. Yet she was more important than anyone else in his life. Could he leave her behind again, even for a short time?

"Okay, okay, okay, I'll hold off on the tickets for now, but let me know the answer soon, man. You have to do this."

When Zack hung up, he didn't move for a few minutes. The old enthusiasm for racing flared. He loved the intense concentration, the smooth working between man and machine. The triumph when he excelled. The cars he drove were masterpieces and could be coaxed to maximum performance by the right skills, which he had.

One more time—for Jacques?

Or was it for him?

One more race, and a challenging one at that, and then hang it up for good. It meant being gone from Rocky Point for a couple of weeks. He didn't need that much practice. He knew that course, he just needed to get to know his new car.

And a bigger percentage would mean an added influx of money. Not that he needed it. He was comfortably well-off. Investments paid nicely. But an extra chunk of change never hurt—especially for his plans to use it if he won.

He'd do it. But he'd wait a day or two before calling Thomas back. Who knew what incentives the man might offer if he waited.

After dinner that night when the expected phone call from Joe came, Zack let Jenny answer it. He had pulled up the information on the Stockholm race and was reviewing the course, mentally remembering all the banks and turns. Focusing on the course, blocking all else from his mind.

"Daddy wants to talk to you," Jenny said a short time later.

"Zack," Joe said when he got on the line. "We've hit a snag."

"With what?"

"Gillian's car broke down when we were ready to leave this morning. Being Sunday, nothing's open, so we have to wait until tomorrow before we'll know what's wrong and how long it'll take to fix. This place is even smaller than Rocky Point, so no telling if the local garage will have any parts needed or the expertise to repair."

"So, what's happening in the meantime?" Zack asked.

"We went to the largest church in town this morning. It was a pretty building, all stone and wood. The people were friendly and the sermon really gave good guidelines for a righteous life. It was after church—we started to leave and only made it seven miles before the car totally died. I've looked at it and am not sure what's exactly wrong with it, but I think it's the fuel pump. I could change it in a heartbeat if I had the tools and the part. But it's old and foreign to boot. Who knows if the local garage stocks the parts."

"Take your time. You don't have a deadline to be home. Once you're on the road again, you can still follow your original plans for seeing the sights."

"I wasn't sure of your timetable," Joe said.

Zack almost told him about the Stockholm race, but held off. For now he needed for Joe to know he was committed to settling back in Rocky Point and could be counted on to watch Jenny.

"I'm not going anywhere. Jenny and I are doing fine. Did you tell her?"

"No. We might be home when planned if we can get it repaired tomorrow."

"I'll tell her. You and Gillian enjoy your trip, take your time, I'm not going anywhere."

For now.

Chapter Five

Marcie glanced at her watch. It was almost nine in the morning. Zack Kincaid would be waltzing into the café as if he owned it about now. Her two waitresses would vie for who served his table. And she'd watch the clock until ten when he'd finally leave. If this was his work ethic, show up late, leave early to get Jenny, she worried for Joe's business. How could they keep up with the demand if one of the partners didn't pull his weight?

That was unfair. She knew from the past both Kincaid men were focused when it came to work. And reliable. Well, in business, anyway. She sighed. She had to stop thinking like that. Zack was a fine, honorable man who had just chosen a different life from the one they'd planned all those years ago. She didn't agree with his choice, or the way he handled it, but that didn't make him anything less than human. People did stupid things—especially when young.

She wished she'd seen the signs back then. But even searching her memory, she could find no clues she'd missed. He'd hidden his feelings so well she'd never suspected.

"Hi, boss. Zack wants to see you," April said from the doorway.

She did not want to see him. It had been three days since she'd caught a glimpse of him leaving church. She was hoping for a full week without being tempted with the sight of Zack Kincaid. Just thinking about him had anticipation spiking, however. Was it too much to wish it would go away?

"Thanks. I'll go out in a minute." Once she had her emotions firmly in check. Taking a deep breath, she smoothed her hair and rose, hoping she could keep this brief.

She spotted him immediately. He was already eating when she stepped from her office into the café. His dark hair had grown a little since he'd been back. She remembered he'd always worn it long when they'd been dating—mostly to get a rise out of his father, as she recalled. Or maybe because she'd once said she liked it longer.

He saw her and smiled, rising as she approached the table. When both were seated, she looked at him, her heart pounding. Frowning at her body's betrayal, she asked what he wanted.

"A favor. A big one, actually." He put down his fork and looked at her. His dark eyes held a beseeching look. She almost said, "Sure," but caution raised its head.

"What kind of favor?"

"You would have said yes in the past."

"I was younger then. What is it?"

"Kimberly has had Jenny over almost every day. The two girls are inseparable. I really appreciate her helping me out that way. I work, pick her up later and don't have to shirk my job or my babysitting responsibilities."

Marcie nodded. "You had to come here to tell me that?"

"No. Jenny asked if we could have Sally Anne over to barbecue on the beach at the foot of the bluff. I'm out of my element dealing with one seven-year-old—I can't manage two. If you'd help out, I'd really appreciate it.

"I'm thinking Friday night, to give Sally Anne's parents an evening to enjoy together, just the two of them. I'd have Sally Anne home by nine. Unless you have a date planned already."

Marcie studied him for a long moment. Was this his way of finding out if she was dating anyone special? Or anyone at all? She was tempted to say she was too booked up to even think of helping out. However, there were no plans. She'd loved spending time on that sandy strip of beach when she was a teenager. She'd even been there several times since

Joe's wife died, helping him with Jenny, enjoying a quick swim when she could bear to be in the cold water.

He didn't say anything further, just held her gaze locked with his.

What was the harm? She could enjoy time with the little girls, enjoy the beach. Enjoy being with Zack again? a small voice whispered.

"Okay. What time Friday?"

"I'll pick the girls up around four. I can swing by and pick you up, as well."

She hesitated.

"It's not like it's a date or anything," he said, clarifying things perfectly. "We'll have two little girls with us constantly. Well, until I take Sally Anne home, then it'll just be one seven-year-old. She's a sweet kid, but sometimes I wonder how to keep up."

"Okay, I'll see you on Friday." When she started to rise, Zack reached out his hand.

"Joe and Gillian have run into problems. Her car died on Sunday and they're still in a small Illinois town awaiting a part. He's frustrated because the local garage won't let him work on her car, and he insists he could fix it in a heartbeat with the right tools. The old man who owns the garage won't hear of it and there's no automotive shop in town to buy the tools, or the part. She drives some foreign car and the man only stocks parts for the most popular American-made cars."

"So what are they going to do?"

"The part's been ordered. As soon as it arrives, it'll be installed and they'll start up again. In the meantime, they're marking time. Can't be driving all around in the rental moving van. Joe says the town gives him an entirely new perspective on Rocky Point."

Marcie laughed. "I bet he's frustrated. Gillian's probably charmed to bits."

"Something like that. Have you known her long?"

"No. Sophie Parkerson died a few months ago. Gillian was her sole heir and showed up the day of the funeral. I met her then. No one even knew Sophie had a great-granddaughter to leave the house to. But we've become good friends. She's a wonderful woman and adores Joe and Jenny. I think she's great for them both."

He nodded, looking pensive.

"And she's happy to live here in Rocky Point, which Pamela wasn't," Marcie continued softly, referring to Joe's first wife.

"So I'm not the only one who's seen the bright lights and can appreciate small-town living," he said.

"We'll see." She rose and smiled politely. "See you Friday. Pick me up at my apartment, please—

I'll leave here a bit early." She was helping out more as a favor to Jenny than to Zack. And she didn't want rumors to start if people saw her with Zack again.

She marched back to her office, proud of the way she refused to turn around to see him one last time when the kitchen doors swung closed behind her. Then she smiled in delight. She'd spend time with Jenny and her uncle and see what more she could learn about the man whom she'd once thought she understood.

And loved dearly.

Friday seemed to drag by for Marcie. She arrived early at work to make sure everything was covered. They were well into June now and tourists were becoming a major part of her business on the weekends. The weather for the next few days was expected to be clear and warm. Another boon to encourage tourism.

She had briefed her manager before returning home early to shower, change and be ready when Zack and Jenny picked her up. Having a few minutes to spare, she called her father. No answer. She left a quick message, wondering where he was. If he'd gone fishing today, he would have stopped before now. The best time was morning, he always said.

Promptly at four came a knock on her door.

When Marcie opened it Jenny bounded in and gave her a hug. "I'm so glad you're coming. Sally Anne and I have been planning this forever. It'll be so much fun. Uncle Zack bought hot dogs and we'll cook them on a fire on the beach. He said he and Daddy used to do that all the time when they were kids."

Marcie smiled. Memories rose of the evenings she'd shared with the Kincaids, and the campfires in the cove beneath their home. The surrounding rock seemed to reflect the heat and they were able to stay out far longer than usual in the cool Maine nights.

Taking a deep breath, Marcie grabbed her jacket and purse and the bag of brownies she was bringing to the feast. She was ready. She was merely chaperoning two young girls. But when she saw Zack leaning against the truck, arms folded across his chest, feet crossed at the ankle, she almost tripped off the steps. He looked amazing, all broad shoulders and masculine stance. His dark eyes watched her, bringing a self-consciousness that unnerved her. Thankfully, Jenny said something about going to pick up Sally Anne at that moment and broke her focus.

"Hi," she said when she reached the truck, her thoughts in a jumble.

"Hi, yourself. Ready? We have to get Sally Anne." He opened the door and tilted the seat forward so Jenny could scramble into the jump seat in the back, then pushed the seat back so Marcie could get in. She brushed past him and climbed in, keeping busy settling herself and pulling on her seat belt so she wouldn't look at him. Okay, this had been a mistake. She was so very aware of every move he made. How would she last the evening?

She should not have worried. Once Sally Anne joined them, the two girls kept a running conversation, including both adults as they jumped from one topic to another.

When they reached the Kincaid house, the girls dashed to the edge of the bluff and waited impatiently for Zack and Marcie.

"This isn't exactly Disneyland," he murmured as they walked across the grassy expanse.

"But enough out of the ordinary to bring excitement. Jenny told me Joe's never had a fire on the beach. She thinks this is amazing."

"What's amazing to me is that he hasn't. We did it all the time, it seems like." Zack remembered his mom and dad directing everything, letting the boys do the work. Marcie had been part of their beach picnics more times than not those last few years before his parents died. At the time, he'd taken it for granted. Now the memories were bittersweet. Great to have, sad to know he'd never share with his parents again.

"But not at Jenny's age, I bet. Until Gillian came,

Joe was very overprotective of his daughter. She's only now allowed to do things other girls have been allowed to do for a while. Doesn't it make you feel special to be the one to introduce her to the joys of cooking hot dogs on the beach?"

He nodded. "Being with her makes me feel special. She sees me as some lost hero."

"Lost?"

"She told me she and her father prayed for me to find my way home, so to her that made me lost."

"So she knows God answers prayers."

"Does He?" Zack asked softly.

Before Marcie could answer, they reached the girls.

"I want to go down first, Uncle Zack," Jenny said, dancing around at the top of the steep stairs that led to the beach.

"Okay, but only if you hold the handrail and go slowly. Sally Anne can follow you and Marcie and I will be right behind you both."

As Marcie descended, she looked at the familiar sheltered beach. It wasn't large, as beaches around this area of the coast went. Sheltered by the rocky bluff that seemed to hold it in open arms, it had limited use, primarily by the Kincaids and their friends. Sophie Parkerson had shared the beach when she was young, but in her last years the steep steps had proved to be too much for her. Gillian had enjoyed the beach a bit since she'd arrived, but it would get the most use during the warm summer months.

She saw that Zack had already laid the wood for a fire, encircled by weathered stones that his parents had carted from the base of the bluff decades ago. The larger ones were to sit on or lean against. The circle of smaller ones were to contain the fire.

There was a cooler nearby, which she suspected held dinner.

Had he missed this when he'd been gone? The carrying on of traditional events? The familiar routines that had been a part of his youth? Had he established new ones in Europe?

"Can we go wading?" Jenny asked, standing near the high-water mark on the sand.

"As long as you don't get your shorts or shirts wet," Zack said with a smile.

With squeals of joy, the two little girls took off their sandals and raced to the edge of the spent wave. Dancing on the packed sand, having the water splash over their feet, seemed to be the height of delight.

"Want to go wading?" Zack asked.

"Sure. Let me put down the brownies."

"I remember you baking a lot when we were teenagers," he said, walking with her to the fire pit.

"These aren't mine. The sisters made them—I

just asked for an extra batch today when they were baking. I don't do much cooking anymore." It didn't seem necessary when she had delicious food prepared for her. And she didn't like to cook for only one. Her meals at home were primarily breakfast foods. Since moving out of her dad's home, she rarely baked anymore.

As the afternoon moved into evening, Marcie realized she was enjoying herself as she hadn't in a long time. The girls kept her laughing. Zack told them stories of some countries he'd visited, and they all hung on his words. Paris came alive; the hectic traffic of Rome had them asking if he raced in the streets. When he spoke of the fjords of Scandinavia, the girls likened them to Rocky Point. When he made light of an act of kindness, she remembered all the more why she'd loved him all those years ago. He had been wild and exciting, but also a kind kid. He'd often done things for Sophie, she recalled. He and Joe had cut her lawn, kept her car in running order. For them it had been fun fiddling with an old car. Marcie knew Sophie had been grateful. Once he'd told her that he considered Sophie a kind of grandmother. Did he know how much his helping her had pleased Sophie?

The hot dogs were a huge success, as was the fire. When they toasted marshmallows on sticks, Jenny declared it the best day ever.

It was growing dark when Zack suggested they head up to the house.

"I don't want to go yet," Jenny said, marshmallow smeared on one cheek.

"I have to lug all this stuff back up—I don't want to do it in total darkness," Zack said.

"We can help," Sally Anne offered.

"How about Zack takes the cooler up and we'll bring the rest," Marcie countered. "And we'll let him go up first and wait until it's almost dark before we go up the stairs."

"Okay," Jenny said. "You can wait for us at the top, Uncle Zack. I know, go get a flashlight from the kitchen, then we can come up with that."

"I didn't hear an offer to help carry the cooler."

"Oh, that's the job of a strong man," Marcie teased. "Not us helpless little women."

The girls laughed at her joke. "We're strong, Aunt Marcie," Jenny said.

"I know, but men like to do things like that to show off how strong they are."

"You know men?" Zack asked.

"A bit about them," she teased. For a moment it was as it always had been between them. Their gazes caught, held.

"You're soo strong, Uncle Zack," Jenny said in false admiration. She and Sally Anne giggled, which broke Marcie's gaze. She laughed with the girls, feeling warmth to her toes.

By the time everyone was at the top of the cliff, it was full night. The sky was darker than normal as the new moon was starting. The stars began to twinkle.

"Can we lie out on the grass and look at the stars?" Jenny asked.

"We need to get Sally Anne home," Zack said.

"I can stay a little while longer. My mom won't care," Sally Anne said.

"You did say you were giving them a night to themselves," Marcie reminded him, surprising herself. She didn't want to leave.

"Do you want to lie out on the grass, getting whatever bugs are around into your hair, probably freezing by the time we're through?" he asked, as though giving Marcie an out.

But she didn't want one. "Where's your sense of adventure? I brought a jacket, the girls can get a blanket from the house and we'll all lie down and look at the stars."

"Okay, I'm overruled, I can see." The smile on his face showed he didn't mind a bit. He locked gazes with Marcie for a moment, surprise shining in his eyes.

The girls yelled with joy and raced into the house to get a blanket. In less than ten minutes, the leftover food had been put away and all four were lying on the blanket, gazing at the dark night sky, Jenny and Sally Anne between them.

"I see the Big Dipper," Jenny said, pointing.

"Me, too," said Sally Anne.

Marcie was content to be near Zack. Share the evening with him, just look at the sky, enjoying the beauty of God's handiwork.

"It's said God knows the names of all the stars," she said softly. "What's that one's name?" Jenny asked, pointing to a bright one near the horizon.

"I think that's Venus," Zack said. "Not a star but a planet."

"Daddy says he always feels closest to God outside. Why is that?"

"Nothing man-made to interfere, I expect," Marcie said.

"So God can hear our prayers better if we're outside?" Sally Anne asked.

"He can hear our prayers wherever we are," Marcie said. "But maybe He hears them a bit louder if we're outside."

"Dear God, please bless my daddy and Gillian and have them come home soon," Jenny said.

As the girls were deep in conversation about the wedding, Zack's cell phone rang. He dug it out of his pocket as he sat up to answer. "What!" he exclaimed into the phone.

Zack's expression was hard to see in the dim starlight. Marcie hoped it wasn't bad news.

"I'll be there as soon as I can get there. Thanks, Tate."

He flipped the phone closed and stood. "Time to take Sally Anne home," he said.

"What happened?" Marcie asked as she scrambled to her feet and helped the girls up.

Zack leaned close to Marcie and whispered, "Sean was picked up with some other teens at a drinking party. When Tate started to call his mother, he asked if he'd call me instead."

"Why?"

"How should I know? But after I drop you and Sally Anne off, I'm heading to the sheriff's office to find out."

"I'll come with you."

Again their gazes locked. And just like that, their evening under the stars was over. But something new seemed to be starting.

After Zack delivered Sally Anne home, he offered again to drop Marcie at her place before heading to the sheriff's office.

She shook her head. "I want to see what's going on. It's not as if teenagers haven't been having keg parties since the beginning of beer," she added. "What's Tate going to do, ground them all for life?"

Zack laughed. "I doubt it. He and I and Joe had a few ourselves." He didn't know why Sean had Tate call him, but the kid could use a break and Zack wanted to find out more about the situation.

"A few what, Uncle Zack?"

Marcie turned and looked at Jenny. "A few experiences they should have waited for."

The little girl looked confused. Zack could see her in the rearview mirror trying to process the adult conversation.

"A friend got into trouble with the law. He called me to help," Zack said.

"Is he a bad man?" Jenny asked.

"No. At least I don't think so. I want to find out what's going on and then help him."

"Jesus would do that, wouldn't He, Aunt Marcie?"

"Absolutely. Do you know if anyone got hurt?" she asked.

"I don't know anything, actually. Will you sit with Jenny while I go in? That'll save me taking her inside."

"Sure."

Zack parked in the lot next to the Town Hall, which housed the sheriff's office in an annex at the back. It was after ten and the streets were deserted. Not a lot of night life in Rocky Point. The lot was well lit, such a contrast to the dark night sky they'd recently been enjoying.

"I'll be back as soon as I can," Zack said, getting out of the truck.

Entering the old building gave him a feeling of déjà vu. He had been the one calling his father one night after he and Joe, Tate and Tom had played some hijinks at the high school. No damage, but the furious principal had called Sheriff Montgomery.

His father had listened to him, explained why Kincaids didn't do things like that and restricted his activities for a month. It had been right when he had first started dating Marcie. Being away from her that month had been the worst punishment he could have had. He wondered if his dad had known that.

The dispatcher sat at one end of the large room, several desks filling the center and rows of file cabinets lining the other wall. A short hall led to the offices, break room and restrooms. The holding cells were in the basement. On a bench opposite the dispatcher's desk sat three teenagers, two unknown to Zack. The third looked up when he entered and then looked away.

Zack nodded at Sean but headed for the sheriff's office. Tate was on the phone when Zack reached the open door. He stayed in the opening, half listening to the conversation. It obviously concerned one of the other boys and sounded as if Tate was having trouble with the person on the other end.

When he hung up he looked at Zack.

"Here for Sean?"

"Do you work all the time?" Zack asked, entering and sitting on the edge of the large old wooden desk.

"No, I was home. Came in when one of the

deputies called. The instigators were sons of some folks visiting. Two of our homegrown boys involved, Sam Tyler and Sean. The kid freaked when I said I was calling his mother. I think he'd rather stay the night in jail than have her come down here. So when he suggested you, I thought, why not?" The sardonic grin Tate gave showed he knew how out of place Zack felt.

"The kid works for me, but I don't really know him."

"I told you before, he's in trouble a bit, but like this, nothing major. Just underage drinking, which I happen to really frown on. He's not had an easy life, so far as I can tell. Want to sign him out?"

"Can I?"

Tate shrugged. "You're not his guardian or anything, but you're a responsible adult, someone I know. And my guess is you might get more out of him than a crying, frantic, overreacting mother."

"Get more what?"

"Information. I want to know who's selling alcohol to minors."

"Code of youth, never tell adults anything."

"Take him home. See what you find out. I'll let the desk know." He reached for his phone and by the time Zack returned to the main room, Sean was standing by the door, still avoiding his eyes. The two other teenagers remained on the bench, an insolent glare for Zack.

"See ya, Sean," one called.

Sean didn't respond.

"Let's go," Zack said, walking past him and out into the night.

Once the door closed behind them, Zack turned and looked at the kid, feeling strange to be in a parental role. Watching Jenny was one thing. This was entirely different.

"So, what's the story?" he asked.

Sean shrugged. "No biggie. So we had a few beers. Grown-ups drink all the time. What's the harm?"

Zack stared at him, not knowing what to say. He didn't want to shut the kid down, but who was he to give advice? *Lord, I need some guidance here.* The prayer came out of the blue. But as Zack studied Sean, he knew it was heartfelt. *Tell me, Lord, what to say to him. How to make him understand how actions at this age can have an effect for the rest of his life.*

"Come over here." Zack went to one of the benches near the sidewalk. It was pretty in the day, sheltered by the shade of the huge oak tree. At night the streetlights were filtered by the leaves, leaving the bench in semidarkness. It was always easier to talk in the dark, Zack thought.

"First of all, alcohol is not the best drink for someone wanting to race. It can rot your brain, wreak havoc with your reflexes, and if you'd been arrested instead of detained, it would be on your record. If you'd been driving and pulled a DUI you could kiss any idea of racing for a legit team goodbye."

"Like I have a chance anyway," Sean mumbled.

Zack leaned back against the bench, gazing into the darkness beyond the street light. "Why's that?"

"I'm stuck in this backwater town, don't have any money or connections. And I have a mother who freaks when I mention racing."

"It's a dangerous profession," Zack commented, thinking instantly of Jacques. "Men can get killed."

"Most don't."

"True. Tell you what, if I can get something put together, we'll have some driving time at that parking lot Tate was telling me about. But only if you stay clean."

"Yeah, not much chance of that changing. These guys tonight, they included me because I had some cash—from working at the café. Normally they don't give me the time of day."

"If you want to learn to race, you need to stay out of trouble, Sean."

"I know." The glum sound in Sean's voice made Zack smile.

"My mom's going to kill me," he continued.

"Well, let's head for home and find out," Zack

said. "My truck's over there. I have to tell you, Marcie's inside."

"What, I interrupted a date? Man, I'm sorry."

"No, we're not dating. My niece is there, too. It's getting late for her to still be up. Come on."

Sean was clearly flustered when entering the truck and taking a jump seat in the back with Jenny. He avoided looking at Marcie, though he did greet her.

"You okay?" Marcie asked.

"Did you get arrested?" Jenny asked, her eyes wide.

"I'm okay and, no, I didn't get arrested."

"What happened?" Marcie said, turning to look at him.

"He got in with the wrong crowd. We'll drop him at home, then I'll drop you off and get this little girl to bed," Zack said.

"I like staying up late, Uncle Zack."

"I'm sure you do. I did, too, when I was little."

When they reached Sean's neatly kept house a few blocks from the main street of Rocky Point, Zack got out with Sean and walked him to the front door. The porch light was on and Marcie had a clear view of the chastened young man and Zack walking with him. At one point he put a hand on Sean's shoulder. She bet he squeezed it.

Sean's mother opened the door and for several moments the three of them talked. Marcie could hear the murmur of voices, but not actually what was being said.

"I'm getting tired, Auntie Marcie," Jenny said. "How much longer?"

"Soon, I think. Your Uncle Zack is talking with Sean's mom."

"I bet he's in big, big trouble. I would be if the sheriff arrested me."

"Yes, you surely would."

Marcie hoped things worked out for Sean. She appreciated his work ethic when on the job. He took extra care and learned quickly. He'd even started to talk to Sarabeth, which seemed to please the older teen.

Zack had been in trouble a time or two as a teenager, and told her about it afterward. His dad had known just the right thing to do to make sure he never repeated the error of his ways. Never busted for the same offense, he liked to brag.

She smiled in memory. Only arrested once for speeding and that was dismissed by the court, but not by his own father. She remembered that restriction—it curtailed their own time together. But he had wild ideas and, at that age, lack of sense. Slowly her smile dimmed. Maybe that was why he'd left as he had. Lack of sense and ability to see a larger picture—such as how it had hurt her, embarrassed her and her father before the entire town.

Now Zack was the wise man in this scenario,

giving advice to a teenager, helping to placate the situation. Thoughtfully she watched as the mother's expression gradually changed from angry to resignation, to hope.

"We should pray for Sean to find his way," Marcie said softly.

"Me and Daddy always pray for Uncle Zack to find his way. Why do they get lost?"

"Sometimes earthly things interfere with the plans God has for us all. *Lord, we ask You to be with Sean and give him wisdom to know what plans You have for him. He's a good worker, Lord. I thank You for sending him my way. May the job he does bring a blessing on him and others. Comfort his mother and give her wisdom, also, please, as she deals with her son. Thank You, Father, for Your love and guidance, amen.*"

"Amen," Jenny repeated.

Zack returned. "Can I call you after I get home and Jenny's asleep?" he said to Marcie.

"Sure," she said, aware of just how much she wanted him to. To hear his voice, to have him reassure her about Sean.

To keep their evening going just a while longer.

Chapter Six

It was almost eleven-thirty by the time the phone call came. Marcie had prepared a cup of hot cocoa and was glancing through the bridesmaid dresses that Jenny had her print out. Which would Gillian like? She hoped one that was Jenny's favorite. It would add another layer in cementing that relationship. Gillian loved Joe's daughter almost as much as she loved Joe. Marcie was delighted with the turn of events.

When the phone rang, she moved to the chair next to it and answered.

"Wasn't as bad as you might have thought," Zack said. "Sean was just trying to fit in. I don't think he's made any solid friends in town. And choosing to go off with these guys was a mistake, but one anyone could make."

"So, what happened exactly?"

"He had money from working at your place and

they hit him up. It was one of the other boys who bought the beer. Tate wants a name so he can get the guy who sells to minors. They were south of town, bragging and drinking and raising a ruckus. Deputy spotted them when on patrol so picked them up. Jason Pullman's been picked up before. I talked to Tate before I called you. He's going to come down hard on Jason, but the others got off with a warning. He said they're not bad kids, just bored."

"I know Sean works well at the café and is friendly with the rest of the staff," she said. "I hadn't thought about the friends angle. How long has he lived in Rocky Point?"

"A couple of years. His father ran out on the family and his mom moved them back here. Mother, grandmother and Sean."

"Ouch, tough for a boy that age to have no father."

"On any age," he said softly.

Marcie sighed. "I know you miss your parents, Zack. But you had them growing up. So how are you going to help Sean?"

"What makes you think I am?"

"The way his mom looked at you when you said goodbye." It had held more hope than Marcie had ever seen in a woman. She smiled. "You're a good man, Zack. What are you going to do?"

"Nothing beyond what I was planning anyway.

He wants to race. At least that's one objective right now. Tate knows someone who has control of that plant over near Monkesville. He's going to see if we can use the parking lot. I thought I'd teach Sean the basics of competitive driving. Skills that won't hurt on highway driving, either."

"A big responsibility."

"Naw, it'll be a piece of cake. Thanks for coming over this evening. Jenny had a great time. She talked about it all the way home."

"It was fun. It reminded me—" She stopped abruptly. She didn't want to go there. It reminded her of many times they'd spent with his family having hot dogs on the beach. Watching the stars.

"Yeah, I know." He didn't say anything for a while. Were the memories happy for him as they had been for her?

"You won't let this stop Sean from working at the café, will you?" he asked.

"No. He works well. You surprised me by taking him home, though," she said. Might as well tell him she admired what he'd done, but the words were hard to say. "I think it was wonderful."

"Hey, my dad helped me out a time or two. This kid just needs some guidance."

"I know. Jenny and I prayed for Sean while we waited. I haven't noticed him at the church. Do you know if he attends Trinity?"

"How would I know? He was at the picnic, though, so probably."

"What about you, will you attend now that you're home?"

"Jenny and I were there Sunday," he said.

"So you'll be making it on Sundays from now on?"

He hesitated. Marcie wondered what he was thinking.

"The thing is, Marcie, I'm not so sure I'm that welcome. Your father isn't happy to see me. Others in town seem to step warily. God's got better things to do than worry about me."

"Zachariah Kincaid, God loves you. He's been watching over you all your life, you know that. I can't believe you'd even say such a thing."

"Well, I didn't do so well by you. One strike against me. I turned my back on my family—even when they needed me. I didn't even come home for Pamela's funeral. Another strike."

"You came as soon as you heard of Joe's burned hands. That wasn't turning your back. And you say you're coming back for good."

"I am."

"Then that means to Trinity, as well." Why was she trying to get him to church? Was it that she wanted things the way they'd once been? Before. So she could excuse her growing interest in the man who had once hurt her so badly? Could she ever believe in Zack again? Enough to try and see him as reliable, dependable—loveable?

"So you don't think God's given up on me?"

"Oh, Zack, don't you remember, He's written your name on the palms of His hands. He loves you. He would never forsake you."

"I need to go," he said, his voice tight with emotion. "Talk to you soon, Marcie."

"Goodbye." But she spoke to a dead phone. *Lord, You know Zack's needs. Please let him feel Your love, let him know You never gave up on him. Could You please, also, give me faith to believe him when he says he's returning for good? And guidance in our relationship. Does that mean we should be friends?*

The next morning Marcie was sampling a new breakfast quiche one of the Cabot sisters had made when April stopped next to her. "Zack is out front and wants to see you."

"Take that with you and go see the boy," Priscilla Cabot said, pushing the plate toward her. "See what he's up to now. Fine-looking young man."

"But unreliable," Marcie said, scooping up the plate and fork.

"He was a kid, cut him some slack, now," she called as Marcie headed to the dining area.

Marcie pushed through the swinging door and

spotted Zack and Jenny at a booth. She joined them, placing her plate down.

"We ordered pancakes," Jenny said after greetings had been exchanged.

Marcie looked at Zack warily. "What's up now?"

"You eating breakfast?" he asked, gesturing to her plate.

"Sampling a new quiche. It's quite good. We'll probably add it to the menu."

"We're heading out to check out that closed mill in Monkesville. Want to ride with us?"

"I'm taking my bike in case I can ride in the parking lot," Jenny piped up.

"Tate's meeting us there with the owner. I thought we could pick up Sean and all go," Zack said.

"You don't need me there. I know nothing about racing."

"So come and learn."

She studied him for a moment. His dark eyes held hers. His smile did weird things to her equilibrium. She did want to go, but for the right reasons? Still—with Jenny and Sean there, and Tate meeting them, how much should she read into the invitation? Probably Zack wanted someone to watch Jenny while he and the others discussed racing.

"Okay, I'll go."

"Yay, I'm glad, Auntie Marcie. You can watch me ride my bike if the man lets me."

"You know, it occurs to me that insurance will

become an issue. Think your dad would talk to me about liability policies?" Zack asked.

Marcie shrugged. She wasn't sure her dad would give Zack the time of day.

Their order arrived and the next moments were filled with getting syrup on pancakes and refilling Zack's coffee cup.

"You can ask," she said, wondering what her father would say. "It could be expensive."

He shrugged. "That's what I need to know. If he won't help, I'll have to go to the competition." The amusement in his eyes told her he was teasing. Still, if her father didn't help, he'd have no other choice.

"When do you need to know?"

"Probably after I talk to the owner. If he's not agreeable to our using the place, I don't need any insurance."

When breakfast was finished, they went to pick up Sean and headed for Monkesville, a short drive inland from Rocky Point.

Sean was quiet in the back. Whether because Jenny chatted nonstop, not giving him a chance to say anything, or because he was still embarrassed about last night, Marcie wasn't sure. She watched Zack drive, his focus on the winding road. Did he want to drive faster? After racing cars at extraordinary speeds, how did he settle to staying just below the posted speeds on the highway?

"What?" he asked, flicking her a glance.

"Just wondering if you wanted to go faster."

"No. I'm enjoying the pace. Gives me a chance to look around. It's pretty countryside, always has been."

When they arrived at the abandoned mill, the gate to the parking lot was open and there were two cars inside. Marcie recognized the sheriff's vehicle from Rocky Point. She presumed the other belonged to the owner's representative.

Introductions were made once Zack and his passengers had left the truck. Hal Norris was representing the firm that still owned the property.

"We aren't sure we want something like you're proposing here," Hal prompted.

"Let me get my niece's bike from the back so she can entertain herself while we talk," Zack said. He quickly set the bike on the ground and Jenny happily rode around, exploring the huge paved parking lot that encircled the plant on three sides.

Marcie noticed Zack took the time to look around, assessing what he saw.

"I understand the mill's been empty for a while. No buyers?"

"Not in this economy," Hal said. He was tall and thin with very little hair. He looked like an old-fashioned accountant, Marcie thought. He'd look complete with a green eyeshade.

"What I propose won't be using the building at

all, just the parking lot. I like that the entire property is fenced—that'll reduce the likelihood of vandalism."

"Oh, we get plenty of that. The windows seem to be targets for guns and rocks," Hal muttered, frowning as he looked at the old brick building. "The longer it sits on the market, the more outdated and problematic it becomes. Still, maybe one day it'll sell. If nothing else, eventually, it'll sell for the land alone. But we're a long way from that point. Come on, let's walk around and you can tell me what you want this for."

Marcie chose to let the men amble around the parking lot while she lowered the tailgate of the truck and sat in the sun, watching Jenny, wondering what caused Zack to want to help Sean to this extent. The huge lot would be perfect for driving training, defensive driving, even drag racing, if properly marked off. Maybe. Where was he finding time and money for this? Was he unable to let the racing go? Was this his way to keep involved?

Such a comedown from grand prix racing. He wouldn't like it. In no time he'd get bored in Rocky Point and leave. She sighed. This time she knew there was no future. As kids, all things seemed possible; now as an adult, she wondered if that were true.

I can do all things through Christ. The familiar verse from Philippians popped into mind. Did all things include getting a certain man to find contentment in a quieter life than he'd lived the past decade?

"This is fun, Auntie Marcie," Jenny said, riding by. "It's so big. Watch, I can ride all the way to the fence and back." She took off, pedaling fast as she went the entire length of the lot. The men were standing near the main entrance to the building, gesturing. She could tell Sean was not contributing, but he seemed to be soaking up every word.

Her gaze was drawn to Zack. He and Tate were the same height, Hal Norris just a bit shorter. But it wasn't only the age difference or size that set the two Rocky Point men apart. Zack had an air of confidence, clearly showing the world that here was a man who knew what he wanted and how to get it. Tate had a similar assurance, in part because he represented the local law, she thought. Or maybe from his years in Boston.

Sean couldn't find better men to associate with. She still wondered why Zack had stepped in. Another man would have let Sean deal with his own troubles last night. She sighed softly. Zack would make an awesome father.

Marcie was starting to grow bored when they finally headed back to the car. A quick glance at her watch told her they'd been here over an hour. What could they talk about all that time? It was a simple proposition—let Zack and Sean use it or not.

"I'll be in touch," Zack said to Hal when they reached the vehicles. They shook hands and Hal and Tate went to their cars. Soon only Zack and Sean stood, still studying the lot.

"So, how did it go? Will this work?" Marcie asked, hopping down from the tailgate.

"Some details to work out," Zack said, looking at Sean. "But I think we have ourselves a course."

The teenager grinned. "Man, that was some discussion. I never knew so much would be involved."

"It's not a done deal, but we're one step along the way. Anyone interested in lunch?"

With a chorus of *I am*s, he smiled and gestured to the truck. "Let's find something here in Monkesville before we drive home."

The hamburger joint they picked offered picnic tables on the side of the property. Once everyone had all they'd ordered, they went to sit in the shade to enjoy the burgers and fries and milkshakes.

Marcie glanced around and noticed others smiling at their group. They probably looked like a family out for lunch, instead of four people from four different families gathered together.

Once seated Jenny piped up, "I'll say grace."

Sean looked startled, but when he saw Zack and Marcie closed their eyes, he followed suit.

The food was delicious. The shade kept the warmth at bay. The two males in the group talked almost nonstop about the prospect of a course. Sounded to Marcie more like an obstacle course than a race course.

When they seemed to wind down, she smiled at Sean. "Do you and your mother attend Trinity Church?" she asked.

"Sometimes," he said.

"We go every Sunday," Jenny said. "And Vacation Bible School starts soon and then we get to go every day."

"Every day?" Sean asked.

"It's for all ages, you should try it," Marcie invited. She looked at Zack. "Remember our senior year, we had basket weaving as our project."

He smiled in return. "Mine looked like a much-used bird's nest."

"At least you finished yours. Mine still had the straw sticking every which way when I got so tired of looking at it, I threw it away."

"Basket weaving?" Sean asked.

"There are crafts as part of the activities, geared to age groups. I guess they thought we'd all learn something about patience doing that project."

"Last year I made a picture frame and we had pictures of our class to go in it. This year Gillian's teaching my grade," Jenny said.

"Who's Gillian?" Sean asked.

"She's going to be my new mom. She's really wonderful."

Sean glanced at Zack.

"My brother's marrying the girl next door. They're moving her things from Nevada now. Be home next week, we hope. They had car trouble."

"And nothing's more frustrating for a car mechanic than to have someone else work on his car," Marcie added. "And to have to wait for parts. Invite your mother to church Sunday. I'd love to meet her."

Sean nodded but didn't say anything.

It was midafternoon when they reached Rocky Point. Zack dropped Sean off at his place then drove to Bill Winter's insurance office. There was a Closed sign on the door.

Marcie frowned. "That's odd. Dad usually stays open Saturdays for those clients who can't see him during the week," she said when she spotted the sign. She got out of the truck and went to the door. The sign simply said, *Closed Saturday. Back on Tuesday.* There wasn't even a phone number to call to get in touch with him. That was unlike her father.

"Everything okay?" Zack asked. He joined her and peered through the glass beside the door. "Office's empty."

"The sign says he'll be back on Tuesday. Wonder where he is."

"Want to run by his place and make sure he's okay?"

She bit her lip in indecision. "I can go after you drop me off."

"I don't mind. It's not as if he lives way out in the country or anything. Come on."

When they reached Marcie's family home, Bill's car was not in the carport.

"No need to get out. If the car's gone, so's he."

"Maybe a fishing expedition?"

"Probably. But much as he likes fishing, he also cares for his clients. He wouldn't normally leave them in the lurch."

"Did he know you were going over to Monkesville with us?"

"No."

"So, you two don't share plans—who knows what he had going today. I'm sure he's fine. Come on, I'll take you home. Unless you'd like to come out to the house, have some more hot dogs on the beach."

"Yes, that's so cool, Uncle Zack," Jenny said from the backseat.

"No, thanks. I need to get some things done at my place. And I want to check in at the restaurant. It's been interesting today. I hope this project keeps Sean on the right path."

"We'll pray for him, Auntie Marcie, won't we, Uncle Zack?"

Zack nodded. "I guess we will."

Marcie grinned and patted his arm then drew her hand back. That was too personal. "Be good for you. And say a prayer for yourself, Zack."

* * *

Marcie freshened up a bit and then walked to the restaurant to see how things were going. Saturday afternoons proved popular with visitors, stopping for a quick snack, or in some cases an early dinner. Her manager was doing well, so she returned home. After starting a load of laundry, she called her father. There was no answer.

She called two of his friends. One was home and had no knowledge of any fishing plans. The other phone just rang and rang. She was beginning to become more concerned. Where was her dad?

When her phone rang, she grabbed it, hoping it was her dad. It was Zack.

"Did you hear from your father?" he asked. She relaxed a bit, realizing how grateful she was that someone else cared.

"Not yet. I called and left a message on his answering machine, but he hasn't called back. And I checked with one of his friends—no big fishing expedition that he knew of. This isn't like him. Usually I can reach him whenever I need him. I hope everything is okay."

"I tried his home, too, but thought he might just be avoiding me. I'm not exactly on his list of favorite people," Zack said.

"Did you call him about the racing plan you have for locals?"

"Actually, I might give some racing pointers, but

now I'm thinking more defensive driving training, how to react to sudden obstacles, that kind of thing."

"You'd know better than most, having had so much experience in Europe."

"I would indeed."

"I don't know what else to do about my dad. I've left messages."

"As soon as he hears one, he'll call. Don't worry. My experience is if it's bad news, it gets around fast, especially in a small town like this."

"Different from Europe, I know. Which city did you like best?" she asked. Maybe hearing about his life away from Rocky Point would give her something else to think about other than her father. A man who left because a town was too pokey wouldn't return after experiencing all the fabulous things foreign cities had to offer.

"Probably Stuttgart. It reminded me a bit of here. No ocean, of course, but the mountains, the hills and the terrain. London's fabulous, too."

Marcie settled back to listen to Zack talk about his life over the past years. So different from hers. She loved hearing his voice. From the descriptions he gave, she could envision the places he'd seen, almost as if she'd been there, too.

He talked a lot about a man named Jacques. Finally she asked him who he was.

"A good friend. We started together. Ended up

competing, of course, but always had time to visit around the circuit."

"Where is he now?"

"He's dead. A freak crash last February. I sometimes can't believe it. But his death put things in perspective." His voice sounded bleak over the phone.

"Like?" She ached for the sorrow she knew he dealt with. He really missed his friend.

"Like, I've spent the last ten years of my life living with strangers, not coming home, not getting to know my niece. Racing's great. I owe a lot of who I am today to that sport, but it's not everything. And certainly not worth dying young."

"So that's why you came home."

"No, I came home because Gillian sent word Joe needed me. I'm *staying* for that reason. Jacques's death hit me hard."

"Won't you miss racing?"

"Might."

She didn't know what to say to that.

"But I'd miss spending time with my family more. Imagine if Jenny had grown up without me even knowing her, or her me. Imagine if I missed time with my brother and another accident happened. Racing is exhilarating, challenging and dangerous. But I never really considered dying young. After Jacques, I have. And there's lots I want to do before dying. Racing has been good to me. I'm comfortably well-off. I can choose how to spend the next ten years and the ten after that and after that. I'm hoping for the old age Sophie had, not the early death of my parents or Jacques."

"None of us know when God will call us home."

"No, so I need to make the most of the time I have, wouldn't you say?"

"There's nothing stopping you from visiting from time to time. You don't race every day of the year."

"True, but there's the danger factor. And the loneliness factor."

Marcie knew about loneliness, but she kept silent. She was not giving him any ammunition to use against her better judgment. She would guard her heart this time against the searing hurt she'd experienced before. Though she wondered if it were already too late. She enjoyed being with Zack, seeing the man he'd become. Knowing he cared enough to rally when family needed him. To even help out a virtual stranger when he had stepped in with Sean.

"Do you think Sean will come to church with his mother? It's a great way to get connected to like-minded people."

"He's been there. I hope he knows he'd always be welcomed. If they come, good and well. If not, it's their choice," he said.

"But you and Jenny will be there, right?"

"Sure."

"See you then." Marcie said good-night and hung up the phone. Trying her father once more before bed, still no answer. She left another message and went to bed, comforted by Zack's assessment that bad news traveled swiftly. If something was wrong, she would have heard by now.

The next morning was gray and drizzly. Marcie drove the short distance to church rather than splash through puddles. The parking lot was filling up fast. She wasn't the only one to drive in this weather. Waving at friends, she dashed into the building and headed for her Bible study class. She'd see her dad later and find out what was going on.

However, when she entered the sanctuary for the morning service, she didn't see her father. Going to the pew they normally sat in, she looked around, wondering if he were sick or something. That would not explain the car's absence from the carport.

Or maybe he had made fishing plans with other friends that his old friend Walt didn't know.

"Hi, Auntie Marcie," Jenny said, slipping into the pew beside her. "I wish it wasn't raining. I can't ride my bike in the rain and Sally Anne and I were going to the park today. Uncle Zack said I could."

"Where *is* your uncle Zack?" Marcie asked, wondering if he wasn't coming.

"He's coming. He had to park the car," Jenny said, and Marcie's anticipation grew.

"This seat taken?" Marcie's dad smiled at her from the aisle. "How're you doing, cupcake?"

"Dad! Where have you been? I was worried sick when I couldn't reach you." She searched his face, looking for any sign of something wrong. He looked the same as always.

"Sorry, I guess I was out of cell service."

"When did you get home?"

"Came straight here this morning. I haven't been home yet." He looked beyond her to wink at Jenny. "Your dad coming home soon?"

"Yes. He calls every night. I miss him."

"I bet you do." Settling back, Bill gazed at the front of the church. The musicians were taking their places; the service would begin shortly.

"We came by your place yesterday, but you weren't home," Marcie said softly.

"We?"

"Zack Kincaid has an insurance question."

From her father's expression, she knew he was not going to take this well. "Are you seeing him?"

"Not really." Well, not *seeing* as in dating. "He asked me to help watch Jenny yesterday, so we all spent the day together." She'd been excited when he'd invited her to join them. She'd seen more of the man he'd become. And liked the way he did things.

"There're other insurance representatives," her father said, interrupting her thoughts.

"But not in town. Come on, Dad, listen to what he has to say, then decide. Never turn away a customer."

"Humph."

"So, where were you yesterday?" she asked. She wanted answers!

"Out and about. The service is beginning."

She stared at him, taking in the more deeply etched lines on his face, the tiredness in his eyes. "Are you okay?"

"Fine."

She eyed him again, but the music began and Marcie picked up her hymn book. As the congregation stood for the opening song, Zack came down the side aisle and made his way to stand beside Jenny. Marcie kept her gaze firmly on her hymn book. Her nerves seemed to hum with his nearness. She was acutely aware of his strong voice when it joined in the singing. How often they'd sat together, harmonized and relished the different hymns, talking after the service about which they'd liked best.

Her father's strong voice was on her left, Zack's on her right. She could hear Jenny's sweet young voice as she raised her own in joyful worship.

When Pastor John finished the sermon some time

later and the final hymn had been sung, Bill Winter stepped quickly into the aisle.

Not so fast, she thought. "Want to have lunch together?" Marcie asked him as she gathered her purse and Bible.

"Sorry, cupcake, I told Walt we could get some fishing in."

"I thought you like early morning fishing."

"On Sunday, I'll take it whenever. Next week for sure we'll have lunch."

He bid Jenny goodbye but refused to look at Zack.

"I'm thinking your father's not going to become my insurance broker," Zack said right behind her.

Jenny squeezed between them and hurried toward the back of the sanctuary to see Sally Anne. With the press of the people moving out, Marcie stepped back out of the flow.

"I'm worried about him. Something's wrong."

He held her gaze, concern in his own eyes. "What?"

"I don't know, but I want to find out."

"If something's going on, wouldn't he tell you?" Zack asked. He longed to reach out and touch her forehead, erase the worry lines, say something that would bring a smile.

"I guess. But I'm not sure. He keeps telling me he's the parent, I'm the child, though I'm all grown up now. But he doesn't want to worry me." She sighed. "It's probably nothing."

"Since he's not taking you to lunch, want to join Jenny and me?"

Marcie was ready to say *no,* but then she looked at Zack. He was close enough that she could smell his aftershave. His dark eyes watched her steadily. He waited patiently for her answer, something in his eyes asking her to say *yes.* And why not? He *was* a nice man. And she adored Jenny. Sunday was her day of rest—she might as well enjoy it.

"Thank you, that would be nice. Did you want to go to the café?"

"I originally thought about trying the sea shanty at the marina. Not in the rain, however. There's only outdoor seating. So, if you're not too tired of your own place, let's go there."

"Okay." They stepped into the aisle and joined the flow to the back. When they reached the vestibule, Zack touched Marcie's shoulder and pointed to the left. Sean and his mother stood watching the crowd mill by.

"They came!" Marcie said, surprise then pleasure showing on her face.

"Let's go say hi."

Marcie glanced at Zack as they headed that way. Together as a couple as they'd once been. She liked it.

Sean's face lit up when he spotted Zack and Marcie coming their way. He spoke to his mother and she smiled.

Introductions were quickly made and the four of them chatted for a few minutes.

"I can't tell you how much your taking an interest in Zack means to me," Earline O'Connell said. "He loves working and earning some money of his own. And knows now to be a good steward of the money and not let fly-by-night friends talk him into anything he knows is wrong," she said with emphasis, nailing her son with a steely look.

"I know," Sean affirmed.

"Would you care to join us for lunch?" Marcie asked.

"Another time, perhaps. My mother's home preparing lunch for us. So nice to meet you."

Marcie and Zack said goodbye and went to find Jenny so they could head for their own lunch.

"She seems nice," Marcie said.

"Nice and probably a bit overwhelmed dealing with a teenaged boy. I know my mother used to feel completely lost sometimes with Joe and me. But my dad would usually just calmly state it was the way of boys."

She looked at him. "And did that work?"

He laughed and shook his head. "Her standards were high and we were expected to meet them."

Marcie privately thought both Kincaid men showed the loving standards their parents had instilled.

The after-church crowd at the restaurant, combined with the summer tourists, had the café nearly full.

"Nice for the owner, not so nice for us," Zack commented when told there would be a short wait for a table.

"It wouldn't be so bad if we could use our outdoor tables. Lots of people like to take advantage of the side terrace when the weather's nice," Marcie murmured, feeling self-conscious standing in line for a table at her own place. She was well aware of the speculative glances when customers saw whom she stood with.

"I like this place," Jenny said, bouncing on her feet. "I want pancakes."

"Didn't you get breakfast?" Marcie asked.

"Yes, but not pancakes. Miss Cabot makes the best ones in the world. Gillian's are good, too," she added as if afraid of betraying a loyalty.

When a table was ready, Marcie led the way, stopping to greet friends and customers as she wound through the crowd. Many of her friends knew Zack and their history. She could just imagine the buzzing of conversation when they passed. Maybe coming here had been a bad idea. She raised her head. She didn't care what others thought. She was happy to share lunch with Zack and Jenny.

While they waited, Marcie and Zack told Jenny how the café had looked when they'd been kids. Zack complimented Marcie on her renovations and then reminded her of the takeaway they'd tried one time. She laughed and caught his look.

"What?"

"Nothing—nice to see you laugh. I've missed that."

Instantly she felt flustered. She glanced away, her heart pounding. When the meal was served, she tried to recapture her composure. Which was threatened yet again when she passed Zack the salt and his finger brushed hers. Taking charge of the conversation, she kept it firmly away from memories and focused on Joe and Gillian's nightly calls, the weather and the proposed driving course.

They had driven their separate vehicles to the restaurant, so when the meal ended Marcie headed for her apartment, not wanting to leave their company. Zack and Jenny were heading home, Jenny still complaining she couldn't ride in the rain.

And Marcie thinking about a dark-eyed man all over again.

"Auntie Marcie's nice, isn't she, Uncle Zack?" Jenny said as they watched Marcie drive away.

"She is."

"And pretty."

More than pretty. Her hair was always a soft shiny brown, satiny to touch, which he remembered from before. Her eyes lit up when she smiled, and he could feel the happiness whenever she laughed. He wanted to be with her, recapture what he'd thrown away.

"That, too." He backed out of the space and headed for the house on the bluff. He'd enjoyed his time watching Jenny, but now he looked forward to some adult-only time—with Marcie. Would she go out to dinner with him if he asked again? Just the two of them. Time would tell.

"You should marry her. She's really nice."

He glanced at the earnest expression on Jenny's face. "You think she'd marry me?"

"You're nice, too," Jenny offered hopefully.

"We'll see."

"Then I could be in your wedding," Jenny added.

Zack burst out laughing. So much for matchmaking. His niece was getting into the wedding mode—anyone's would do. But he couldn't stop thinking about the wedding they'd almost had. And what it would be like to be married to Marcie Winter.

Chapter Seven

Zack turned in the driveway, the gray house with its white trim blending in with the gray drizzle, making him restless.

The phone was ringing when they entered. Zack went to answer as Jenny went upstairs to change into play clothes.

"Zack, man, have you decided? You're killing me, man, with the suspense." His team leader's voice came through loud and clear.

"I'll do it. But just the one race, Thomas. I'm not returning for good. I've got a few things going on here and can't be away long."

"Hey, a couple of weeks to get the feel of the track and the new car, and you'll be ready to win the race. Then we'll talk."

"No more talk. I said I'd do this one, but it's the end. And any money I win goes to Jacques's parents, got that? I've given it a lot of thought since your call." Jacques had been their only son, only child. And Zack wanted to make sure they knew how much he'd meant to him.

"Hey, man, whatever you say. We'll meet you in Stockholm in two weeks. Two weeks, a week later we'll be riding into the winner's circle. We're staying in the Olgatha Hotel near the track."

"I'll see you then." Zack hung up. Once Jenny was asleep he'd call for plane reservations. He flexed his hands, imagining the feel of the wheel, already thinking about the turns of the course— one of the most challenging designs in the circuit. The adrenaline began pumping as he envisioned himself pushing the new car to the limit. He did like the speed and the control he could command over the machine. He always had.

Wednesday evening Marcie was home when the phone rang. She picked up, surprised to hear Gillian on the other end.

"Where are you?" she asked.

"We're home! It took forever to get my car fixed. And we've been away from home so long, I just wanted to come straight back. We'll go see Chicago and New York another time. How have you been? Jenny said you've been to the house and went on a visit to Monkesville with Zack. Tell me what's going on."

"We have settled on a tentative friendship, I

guess. It's hard to avoid each other in such a small town. And with Jenny."

"He was a love to watch her for us. I just hope it wasn't too awkward dealing with him."

Dare she share with Gillian how her feelings were growing for Zack? That's what might prove awkward, since Gillian would soon be Zack's family.

"Tell me about your trip and how it feels to be back," she said, deciding to hold off a bit longer. And maybe see if she could quantify her own feelings better before telling Gillian.

Marcie smiled as her new friend went on and on about her love for Rocky Point and the new friends she'd made. When talk turned to the wedding, Marcie felt a pang of envy. She shouldn't. She was happy for Gillian and Joe. But it did bring confused feelings. Maybe Marcie wasn't as ready for friendship with Zack as she thought.

"One evening next week we need to review where we are so far," Gillian said. "Oops, gotta go, the guys are putting things in the wrong rooms."

Marcie hung up slowly and then bowed her head.

Heavenly Father, please remove the envy from me. I want to only rejoice for my friend in her happiness. Not everyone needs to be married. But if You see the way clear, and I know You do, then maybe send a hint to me of what I should do. Bless Gillian and Joe, and may their marriage be one of loving happiness.

Her office phone rang midmorning and when she picked it up, it was Gillian again.

"Sorry to bother you at work. I wanted you to come vet the renovations Joe and his guys did on my studio. I'll call in a lunch order from the café and if you bring it down, we can eat and talk. And you can tell me how it strikes you—as a possible client."

"Sounds like a plan, and let lunch be my treat. I'll be there around one."

The rain from earlier in the week had ended, leaving the summer day clear and fresh. Marcie enjoyed walking along Main Street toward the sea. Joe Kincaid had his automotive restoration shop right near the water and had rented space in a second building he owned to Gillian for an aerobics studio. Marcie had been one of the first to sign up and was excited classes would be starting soon. Gillian had had the place painted, some walls installed and the bathroom renovated. At one time she thought she might even be living in the apartment above the studio, but Joe's proposal and the resolution to her inheritance had changed all that.

When she opened the door to the studio, Marcie was instantly impressed. It looked amazing. The walls were a light yellow, bound to be bright and cheery even on the rainiest days. The hardwood floors gleamed. There were mirrors along one long wall, pads stacked up and stair step equipment along another wall. The big picture windows on the street had been frosted partway up for privacy, while letting in all the light.

"Hi," Gillian said, coming from a back room. She ran to give Marcie a hug and then turned and swept her arms wide. "What do you think?"

"It looks amazing."

"Come on in the back. It's so nice. Joe got me some furniture for my office, including a small conference table where we can eat." As they headed to the rear of the building, Gillian looked at her with a considering look. "How are things going with Zack? Is it really awkward?"

"It was at first. Now sometimes I forget he's been away. Not that I think he's going to stay." She wished she could believe he would. He was constantly in her thoughts. She even caught herself counting the minutes until she could see him again.

"Yeah, I know. Sit down. I don't know him very well, but he seems preoccupied most of the time I've been around him. Like he's sad or something. I guess he's missing racing."

"A friend of his was killed a few months ago. He's still grieving," Marcie said, frowning. "I don't know much but that Jacques was a close friend. His death is one reason Zack's back. I wish I could help, but he keeps things bottled up. He did when his parents died, too." Just being around him back then seemed to help. Now she wasn't sure. She opened the bags she'd brought and spread the lunch out. She'd opted for a shrimp salad with crusty Greek bread, iced tea and individual apple crisps the Cabot sisters had made for today's special.

"I'm sorry to hear that," Gillian said, quiet for a moment. "The food looks amazing, Marcie. Thanks."

"Always out to please the customer. Where are the Kincaid guys today?"

"Joe's back at work. You should have seen how frustrated he was not to be able to fix my car the minute it died. Zack was going in, too, something about a teenager they have interning there this summer."

"Interning?" Marcie laughed. "He's also working at my place for cash. Sean O'Connell. Nice enough kid. Fascinated with Zack."

"Zack seems to think he's interested in racing."

"Maybe that, too, but to see them together, you can tell Sean really hangs on everything Zack says. Which is good, but odd in a way."

"In what way?"

"I didn't see Zack Kincaid as a mentor," Marcie said.

"Umm." Gillian finished her mouthful before replying. "Do you think you see him as he was, and maybe not as he now is?"

Marcie stared at her as she considered that. "Maybe. He's not quite as wild as I remember."

"I know it must have hurt horribly when he left. I think it's nice you even give him the time of day," Gillian said.

"It's been ten years." Not that there was a time limit on some hurts.

"Some hurts never completely go away," Gillian said.

No, they don't, Marcie thought, though lately a new interest in Zack was replacing the old hurt. "Enough of me. Tell me about opening for classes. When?"

Gillian started in with her plans for the near future, working around the upcoming Vacation Bible School and then time off for the wedding and honeymoon. Her plans were to ramp up to a full schedule by mid-September. School would be in session, summer tourists gone and local residents ready to start a new routine, at least that was her hope.

"Any advice you can give would be welcomed," she said, winding down. "You've had a very successful business for years."

"I've been blessed. We could pray before the opening, asking God to bless the business, the proprietor and all those who partake of the benefits."

"Perfect. That'll be next week. I'm calling everyone today who already signed up. In your case, here's your personal notification—the first class will be Monday at 2:00 p.m. You indicated afternoons would be best."

"I can always get away for an hour or so. I can't wait."

"Now, the next subject. The wedding."

The two discussed the plans for the reception, to be held in the church fellowship hall. Marcie was catering the event and the menu had to be finalized. She offered Gillian and Joe a tasting, sampling all the various items that could be supplied. "It's like a preparty," Marcie said. "I've done it for a couple of other weddings I've catered. Sometimes the entire wedding party attends. That's up to you. Jenny would love it."

"I would, too. We could invite everyone, so they get to meet each other. I'm thinking the matron of honor and best man."

Marcie laughed. "Zack will be surprised, I bet."

Gillian nodded, mischief in her eyes.

When Marcie left to return to the restaurant, she impulsively turned the opposite direction, which would take her past Joe's shop. The big roll-up doors were raised, letting all the fresh air and ocean breeze sweep through. Three vintage cars stood on blocks, two being worked on by two men, another man at a workbench. She spotted Zack with Joe, heads bent into the engine compartment of an old car. She wished she knew makes and models and could identify the car. She loved the long flowing lines. It had obviously been well cared for over the decades. Soon it would purr as it had on the first day it was made.

For an instant she felt transported back to the garage at the house on the bluff where she'd spent many afternoons watching Joe and Zack, bent over cars, revving engines and thoroughly enjoying themselves.

"It's nice you can make a hobby a paying business," she said.

"Hey, Marcie, good to see you." Joe wiped his hands and gave her a hug. "Have you seen the studio?"

"Just came from there. It looks amazing. I can't wait to start up."

"Gillian says soon," Joe said, flicking a glance at his brother.

Zack had also straightened, and was now wiping his greasy hands. He'd said a quiet hi, his gaze concentrated on the towel.

"How are your hands?" Marcie asked, conscious of Zack's silence.

Joe held them up, palm out. "All healed. It sure took longer than I wanted. I think the oil and grease from the cars is helping them heal."

"Yuck, couldn't you just use some hand lotion?" Marcie said, wrinkling her nose.

Joe laughed. "Not the same. Need something?"

Zack leaned against the car and watched her.

"No, just stopped to say hi now that you're home." She looked at Zack. "Did you ever connect with Dad about insurance?"

"No. I figure he's not going to do business with me no matter what, so I'll call around in Monkesville."

She bit her lip. She knew her father was still angry about the way Zack had left things in the past, but business was business.

"I'll swing by his place on my way back to the café and see what's going on."

"Don't put yourself out," Zack said. "I can take a hint. He's not going to be happy if I stay around."

"If? I thought you said you were." Marcie felt the shock to her toes. She was just getting used to the idea of Zack staying, and now it sounded as if he might not.

"Yeah, well, some things came up."

"He's going back to Europe for a race," Joe said neutrally.

Marcie forced a smile. "How nice. Then I won't have to bother about the insurance. You won't be here to do anything about it anyway." She turned.

"It's just one race," he said, walking to catch up with her and keeping pace as she left the garage.

"Sure, one and then another. Don't worry about a thing, Zack. This time there's nothing between us, so why not go back to what you love?"

"It's not like that. It's just one race. I've told them that's the end. The new driver for the team isn't working out. There are a lot of people earning a living off my racing. I can't leave them in the lurch."

Why did it feel like her heart was breaking all over again? "No need to explain."

He reached out and stopped her with his hand on her upper arm, gently swinging her to a halt to face him. "Marcie, I'm coming back. I'm not leaving for good, just for one race at the end of the month. I'll be gone two or three weeks, tops."

"Okay."

"You don't believe me," he said, dropping his arm.

"It doesn't matter what I believe. You might even believe it at this moment. But once there, once back with the excitement and glamour we don't have in Rocky Point, you might change your mind."

"No, I told you, after Jacques's death, I've done a lot of thinking. I want a future. I want ties and roots and permanence."

She looked away. She'd wanted that, as well. But that dream had been smashed. "I've got to go." She glanced at him and took off toward the café. This time he did not go with her.

As she passed the street her father's business was on, she turned down it. It seemed as if it was harder and harder to see her dad anymore.

"Hi, Betty, is my father in?" she asked, entering the front room of the small office.

"Hi, Marcie. No, he's off to Portland again. Did you need something?"

Marcie shook her head, wondering why her father was going to Portland again. Hadn't he been there just last week? What was going on?

"Is everything okay?" she asked.

Betty smiled and nodded. "I can hold the fort. It's slow this time of year."

"When will he be back?"

"I'm not sure. He just said expect him when I see him."

Marcie returned to the café, wondering what was going on with her father. Time she cornered him and found out.

Closing her door when she reached her office, she went to sit at her desk, letting the full emotion of disappointment wash through her. Zack was leaving. Granted, she never thought he'd stay forever. But she was still floored by the revelation. Once back in Europe with all the exhilaration of racing, he'd stay.

Not that it would change things for her that much. Life would go on.

Just maybe in the secret places in her heart she'd

hoped he'd remain in Rocky Point. Hoped that maybe, if she could garner the courage, they would have a second shot at a future together.

"Father, please remove foolish dreams from my mind. Let me focus on what I have and the bless-ings You have bestowed on me and forget what I want. Thy will be done," she prayed softly. When it felt as if a burden had been lifted, she plunged back into the work awaiting. Still thinking about Zack.

Zack returned to the garage and frowned at his brother. "You didn't have to blurt that out to Marcie. I was going to tell her."

"I didn't realize it was a secret. When were you going to tell her? I never knew you two were seeing each other again."

"We're not. Exactly."

"Well, then what, exactly?"

"She's a lot more cautious than she used to be," Zack said slowly.

"Do you blame her? Man, you still don't know how mean that was, the way you took off? Women set a lot of store with weddings and marriage. And you blew it off as if it were a fishing date."

"I called her, told her. I thought I'd come back for her. We would have been together. Only by the time I could afford that, she had her café and you said she was happy."

"She is. Leave her alone, Zack. You're not staying."

"Why does everyone say that? I am. At least if we go partners and I can find a place to live. Otherwise, I'll have to look around Monkesville for a home. But I'm not leaving."

"Except in a couple of weeks."

"That's an exception."

"How many times will you make an exception?" Joe asked.

Zack stared at his brother, wondering if he were right. When Thomas had called, he'd felt the instant thrill that went with racing. Would he always be torn—family and stability against excitement and thrills?

"Looks to me as if you're not certain. Maybe you should pray about that."

Zack turned away. That was the answer he'd get from Marcie, too. If she'd speak to him again. He went to the car they'd been working on, but didn't really see the engine. He didn't know if God would help him out. He'd sort of turned his back on his creator in the past. But this wasn't the past. If people he loved and respected thought the Lord would help him, maybe he should give it a shot. Slowly he bowed his head and closed his eyes.

Lord, it's me, Zack. I'm sorry for so much.

How I've handled my life. How I'm still stumbling through. If You're listening, I'd appreciate it if You would consider helping me out. He waited a moment after the silent prayer, but nothing happened. Had God heard?

Or was he too late?

Please, help Marcie to understand and forgive, he added.

Marcie called her father after she got home from work.

"Hi, cupcake, what's up?" he asked.

Okay, enough was enough. "I came by the office today to see you, but you were in Portland."

"Business. Betty said you'd been by. Did you come to visit or was there something else?"

"Zack's leaving," she said in a rush. Then closed her eyes. That was not what she'd wanted to say.

"We knew he wouldn't stay," he said gently.

"He keeps saying he's going to, but now he's leaving in a couple of weeks for another race."

"Stay away from him, cupcake. He's already proved he's not for you."

"You'd think I'd learned my lesson by now," she said. "Did he call you about insuring a driving scheme he came up with?"

"Betty relayed the message. I didn't call back."

"He's still talking about it. Said he was going to find an insurance agent in Monkesville."

"It's a free country. When I think about it, a driving school is a good idea. Give the kids hands-on experience before they take to the road. I bet lots of folks would like to learn techniques from a winner like he's been. But the draw would be his presence. If he's off racing in Europe, not much scope here, I'd think."

"If he pursues it, Dad, sell him the policy. Don't turn away from business because of what he did when still a kid."

"Sounds like you're standing up for him."

"Not really. But I'm trying to see things as they are now, not as they were. We were so young."

"You're happy now, aren't you?" her father asked.

"Yes." Just longing to be part of a couple. Longing for kids for a grandpa to spoil. "I'm fine. You are, too, aren't you?"

"Of course, why wouldn't I be?"

Marcie hung up, not reassured. She sat by the phone for a minute, then picked up to dial Zack. He answered.

"I thought Joe might answer," she said when she heard his voice.

"He and Jenny are over at Gillian's rearranging furniture, deciding on which room Jenny will have after the wedding, what color to paint the walls. What's wrong with white walls?"

Marcie laughed. "Nothing, they're just boring. I called my dad and he seemed to think you could do well opening a driving school, with your racing wins and all. But only if you stayed."

"Which I plan to do. But you know what? I'm not saying that anymore. I've told you and Joe until I'm almost hoarse. In ten or twenty years, maybe you'll believe me. So does that mean your dad would be interested in insuring such a venture?"

"Maybe. Give him another try. He was in Portland again today." Marcie had enough trust to believe he was staying. Why couldn't she just take him at his word? It was fear of believing him and then being hurt again if he took off.

"Doing?"

"I don't know and he won't say. I'm worried."

"Ask him," Zack suggested.

"I have, and he says everything is fine. But I don't think so."

Zack was quiet for a moment, then said, "If you like, I could try to follow him the next time he goes, see where he's headed. He could have found someone, you know. Are you ready for that?"

"You mean a love interest?" Marcie hadn't thought about that. Her mother had died when Marcie was little. Since she'd moved into her own place five years ago, her father had lived completely alone. He was probably lonely. How *did* she feel about him getting married again?

"That's what I mean," Zack said.

"I hadn't thought about it. I guess I'm okay with

it, as long as the woman is as nice as my dad. He's probably been lonely since I moved out." She hadn't thought about that before. Yet he usually seemed happy enough when she saw him.

"He's not all that old, either, mid-fifties," Zack said.

"I know. I would be selfish if I stood in his way. I want him to be happy. But I don't know about your following him. First of all, I feel like that's spying. I shouldn't spy on my dad. Plus, if he sees you, he'll get that much more angry."

"It was a suggestion, that's all."

"Maybe this is just one of those life lessons about being patient. If nothing's wrong, I'm worried for nothing. And if there is something wrong, I'll have to be patient and wait for him to tell me."

"Is he healthy?"

"I guess, why?'

"He looks thinner than I remember."

"He's older now, too, Zack. You've been gone a long time," she said gently.

"True." He was silent for a few seconds, then asked, "Want to go for a walk?"

"Now?"

"It's not that late. We could walk up and down Main Street and you can fill me in on what every shopkeeper's been doing since I was last here."

Marcie thought about it for a moment. It was not

even eight o'clock. And still warm from the day's heat. "Okay, sounds interesting."

"I'll pick you up in about fifteen minutes." He hung up and Marcie gently replaced the receiver.

She hurried to the bathroom to brush her hair and check her makeup. She should not be spending more time with Zack. Especially now that she knew he was leaving soon for the racing circuit again. Yet, maybe she should grab all the memories she could before he left. Would they have to last another ten years before she saw him?

Pausing in brushing her hair, she stared at herself in the mirror. Where would she be in another ten years? Would she meet someone to love, to marry and start a family with? Or would she still be running a café, catering memorial events and being lonely in the evenings?

Never alone, though, Lord, am I? Let me enjoy my blessings and not constantly long for other things. Show me the path You have for me and let me follow it joyfully.

Marcie picked up a light jacket and was ready when Zack knocked. Slinging it on, she went to open the door.

"Hi," he said, smiling at her in that lazy, heart-stopping way he had.

"Hi." She felt as flustered as she would on a first date. This was Zack. And this was not a date.

They went down the stairs and around to the

front of the building, situated about midway down Main Street. The bakery was closed, of course, but the windows illuminated displays of breakfast rolls and luscious desserts.

"Martins still own the bakery," she said.

"Did Sam go into business with his folks?" Zack asked.

"Nope, he's a vet in Portland. But his cousin Damon came a few years back and loves baking. He'll probably take over when the older Martins are ready to retire. He's nice. His wife sings in the choir."

They slowly walked along the sidewalk away from the sea. The bakery sat almost in the center of town. By going to the end on this side, they could cross over, stroll along the other side to the sea, and then return on the first side to Marcie's apartment. Main Street ran east to west with one end terminating at the sea. The warehouse where Joe had his auto shop had once served as storage for the whaling ships that had plied the seas in the eighteen hundreds. The block beyond Marcie's place held the Johnsons' hardware store.

"You'd think Tate would want to take this on," he said. "Safer than police work."

"He loves being a cop. And his folks are not any older than my dad, still plenty of time for him to consider taking it on when they retire. But I think he'll stick with police work," Marcie said. "He gave up Boston to return home when his father was so sick. But he didn't leave when he got better, which is good for Rocky Point."

"Hmm. So he can return, but you doubt me?"

She looked up at him. "It's totally different. Was this stationery store here before?"

"No, this shop used to be Hanson's Tobacco Store."

"Oh, yes. He moved away about eight years ago. Sales were really poor as fewer and fewer people are smoking. I can't remember where he went, but Stella Lewis owns it now and carries a range from business forms to lovely stationery."

They crossed the side street and continued to the block where the café was situated.

"Tell me about getting the café," Zack said.

"I went to work for the previous owner, remember Oscar Wentworth? With only a high school degree, I didn't have a lot of marketable skills."

"Grumpy old man," Zack murmured.

"He was. And stingy to boot. But he freely shared information about all sorts of aspects of the business—as long as I asked. And I did. I must have pestered him to bits, asking about everything from suppliers, to sanitation, to how to guestimate how many people would be here, to know how much to cook. After a year or so, he gradually increased my responsibilities until one day, out of the blue, he asked if I wanted to buy him out. He was planning to go to Florida and spend the rest of his days in warmth. I think it was just after a really bad nor'easter."

"So you did, buy him out, right?"

"With some help from the bank, of course. That's where living in a small town helped me. Mr. Jarvis was willing to take a risk on me. And I'm happy to say, I've paid back the loan in full."

"You must be doing very well. I hear that restaurants especially have a high failure rate."

"Not when one is practically the only place to eat in town," she said with a grin.

"Except for the sea shack."

"But eating at a bar or at tables outside gets old. And their menu is very limited."

"Do you want to expand?" he asked, studying the café for a moment. "You could take some room from the parking lot."

"No, I have the patio for nice weather dining and the rest is a perfect size for the locals year round."

They crossed the street and continued down the other side, Marcie feeling like a love-struck teenager all over again.

"We should have an ice cream," Zack said, looking down toward the sea. When they'd been dating in high school, he remembered summer evenings when they'd walk up and down the street, commenting on displays, and eating ice cream.

"McFersner's moved. It's across from the barbershop now." If Marcie remembered their former walks, she wasn't bringing them up.

"But still offer those humongous banana splits?"

"Of course. Where else would high school boys ever get their fill of ice cream?"

Marcie continued updating Zack as they passed the cleaners, and the old hotel that so many tourists stayed in because of its charm. The only bar in town she passed swiftly, loud music and smoke drifting out from the half-open door.

"Old man Hendricks still run the bar?" Zack asked.

"Yes, and I wonder how old he really is. When we were kids, I thought he was about a hundred. He doesn't look any older now."

"Probably pickled and smoked to last a long time."

"Umm. He's good about keeping kids out, however. Either because he wants to, or Tate put the fear of the law in him."

It wasn't long before they passed the bank and the hospice thrift shop and reached the large park that overlooked the marina. Zack led the way to a bench that gave a view of the sea in the day. With dusk falling, the water looked cold and uninviting.

"I feel talked out," Marcie said, sitting several inches away from him.

"Some things have changed, but not a lot. In a way, I'm surprised more didn't change over the years. It's nice to find so much the way I remember it."

"Probably seems boring to you."

"No, it seems like home." He gazed at the marina, a thousand memories crowding in. Most of them centered around Marcie. It was good to be back. Seeing things with a different perspective had a way of changing everything. He welcomed Rocky Point and all it stood for.

They sat side by side for a while, letting the tranquility of the sea washing against the pilings seep into them. Gradually the night sky grew darker, the stars began to twinkle. Street lights behind them gave a soft warm glow.

"I've missed you," Zack said, reaching out to take her hand. It was easier in the dark, so he couldn't see her if she pulled back. Instead, Marcie returned his hold, squeezing slightly.

"You've been too busy to miss anyone," she said.

"You're wrong. Especially at night, in some hotel room, or the flat I've called home. No old friends to call and talk to. No buddies to go out with, no special person to share my life with. I threw away a lot for the hope of a dream. I'm not sure it was worth it."

"Oh, Zack, I think God had a wonderful plan for your life. It didn't include staying in Rocky Point. I've had years to think it through. I still have trouble with the way you left. I thought we were so close we could almost finish each other's thoughts. I had no idea you were feeling anything but longing to get married. I read everything wrong."

He turned to look into her eyes. "Not everything. I loved you, Marcie. Really loved you. It was just—I don't know, the feeling I was settling down before the age of twenty and would never go anywhere or do anything grabbed me by the throat and scared me to death. My dad and mom had a great life, but they never went outside of Maine, I don't believe. I didn't want that at eighteen. I handled it wrong. But honestly, if I'd faced you and you'd started crying, I would never have been able to pull away."

Marcie didn't say anything. Zack wanted her to talk to him. Before—ten years ago—they'd talked the night away. Now, nothing.

"Say something," he urged.

She hunched her shoulders a bit, as if withdrawing. Sadness filled her eyes. "I cried so much after you left. Now I just want to think it was worth it. I would feel awful if we lost what we had and neither of us had anything to show for it. I have a nice life here, Zack. God has blessed me in many ways."

"You never married."

She shook her head, looking away.

"Why not? I can't be the only man in the world who sees all you have to offer. Why not, Marcie?"

She pulled her hand away and stood.

"I need to go home," she said, turning to head back up Main Street.

"Why not?" he persisted, rising to stand beside her.

"Because I never found another man who felt like he was the other half of me," she whispered before hurrying away.

Chapter Eight

"The other half of me." The words echoed in Zack's mind as he drove home, as he tried to sleep. They had been so close. It had been like cutting off an arm or something when he'd left. He could relate to the words. Marcie had once seemed to be the other half of him. A half he'd destroyed and thrown away. Seeing her every day, talking to her, he realized he still loved her. She was still the other half of him. The thought had him wide awake. He loved Marcie, probably always had. How could he have been blind enough to think he could ever walk away from her and find any kind of joy in life?

Giving up on sleeping, he rose and went to the window overlooking the darkened landscape. His bedroom from childhood. He'd come full circle. Looking at the starry sky, he offered up another prayer.

Father, guide me, please. Let me make amends

*for the harm I've done. Grant me a bright future—
with Marcie, if that's Your will. I still love her. How
can I convince her of that? I pray You will show
me the way. Thanks for arranging things so I came
home. I'm feeling a bit like the prodigal son. Not
that everyone is throwing a party for my return,
but I know how that guy felt when he returned to
all that was familiar and dear. If Marcie's right
and You did inscribe my name on Your palms, let
me come back to You, as well. Let me be the man
You might always have wanted me to be.*

The peace that descended felt like a hug directly
from God. He smiled. When he slipped into bed,
he had no trouble falling asleep.

The next morning when Zack entered the shop,
Joe and the rest of the men had already started
work. Even Sean beat him in. If he was going to
buy in to the business, he had better show a better
example of punctuality.

"Banker's hours?" Joe said with a grin.

"Needed to work a bit on the track situation. I've
got an insurance man looking into coverage. And
a possible firm who will line the parking area like
I want. Once I get a few more things settled, I'll
head back to negotiate with the owners."

"You're not the only one to have two things going
at once. I think I have a tenant for the apartment
over Gillian's studio."

"I thought you said no one was interested."

"It's been available for almost a year. Today Doctor Mallory sent a referral over. A new nurse for the clinic. She liked it and said she'd be back in touch in a day or two. Apparently she's also looking at a place out on Clinton Road."

"This place would be better in winter. She could walk to the clinic if the snow's too deep to drive in."

"I'm hoping that'll sway her. Plus the view."

"Things are looking up, then." Zack glanced over to Sean. "He's still doing well, right?"

"A natural. Always asking questions. I think nights he's studying classic cars on the internet or something. He really knows more than I expected."

Just then the teenager gave a yell. All eyes turned to him as he pulled his hand out of an engine, a screwdriver stuck through the palm.

"Oh, no," Joe said, rushing over.

Zack was only one step behind. Swinging by the stack of clean rags on a workbench, he quickly wrapped the hand, trying to staunch the flow of blood, letting the screwdriver stay in place to help stem the blood.

Sean looked dazed. "I was trying to force that head off but it was stuck. Shouldn't we pull it out?" He looked at his hand in horror.

"Not yet. It'll help staunch the flow of blood," Zack said. "Come on, I'll drive you to the clinic."

"I'm going, too," Joe said, slinging an arm around the teenager.

In less than five minutes they walked into the clinic that served the town and surrounding area. Dr. Mallory was on duty and quickly assessed the situation.

"I'll get it out, but in case of nerve damage, I don't want to do more than stop the bleeding at this point. He needs the hospital in Portland. I'll call for an ambulance."

"I'll be okay," Sean said through gritted teeth. Zack knew the hand had to hurt, but the kid showed courage, keeping his cool. "I don't need an ambulance."

"Better if a specialist sees this," Dr. Mallory said.

"I'll take him up. No need for the expense of an ambulance," Zack said, guessing some of the reasons for Sean's resistance.

"I'll pack the wound, put on some ice. The sooner you get there, the better," the doctor said.

"I'll go as fast as the law allows," Zack said. Speed was important, but so was safety.

"Hmm, maybe get Tate to drive. He can run that siren and really make time. Watch him for shock, too."

"Okay."

Once on the road, Zack in the back with Sean, Tate really opened up the police car. The highway was not crowded and so he made good time, faster than the posted speed, but still within safety limits.

"Our drag-racing days paid off," Tate said at one point.

Zack grinned. "Who'd have thought? Remember this the next time you find some teenagers speeding along."

"I want to keep them safe."

Sean gave a soft moan.

"Hurts now, doesn't it?" Zack said sympathetically. "The initial reaction's passed and now the pain starts. Those pills the doc gave you will start to work soon. Hang in there, kid."

"If I have to stay in the hospital will you call my mom?" Sean asked.

"We'll call her now," Zack said. He dialed the number Sean gave him and in a couple of seconds heard a woman's voice.

"Mrs. O'Connell, this is Zack Kincaid."

"Didn't he show up this morning? I told him to get up in time. He was up late last night on the computer, so probably slept through this morning."

"Actually, he beat me into work. There's been an accident." Zack explained what was happening then handed the phone to Sean so he could reassure his mother. She insisted on getting to Portland as soon as she was able. Zack took the phone back and told her which hospital they were going to, and that he'd take care of Sean until she arrived.

"I can manage," Sean said, hearing that comment.

"A friend hanging around doesn't hurt," Zack said when he ended the conversation.

"Could you also call Miss Winter for me? She'll be expecting me at two. I hate to let her down," Sean asked.

"Marcie'll understand." Zack made that call, giving a brief recap and promising to call her once they knew what the doctors at the hospital said.

Once they reached the hospital, Zack went in with Sean while Tate went to park the car. The emergency room was quiet. They were able to take Sean immediately, and Zack was told to wait until after they went to X-ray, and returned before going in with Sean. He nodded, understanding the drill, and went outside to find Tate. Wandering around the side of the building, he came to the general parking and saw Tate wending his way through the parked cars.

The doors marked Outpatients whooshed open to his right and out walked Bill Winter, Marcie's father. Zack did a double take and the older man stopped suddenly, then looked as if the world had fallen in.

"Don't you tell Marcie!" Bill said with a stern note.

"What's going on?"

"Nothing you need to be concerned with. What are you doing here anyway? Did you follow me?" he asked suspiciously.

Zack studied the doorway behind him speculatively, then looked at Bill. "We had an accident at the shop and I had to bring Sean O'Connell in to the E.R. Shouldn't Marcie know about this?" Zack didn't have a clue what her father was doing here, but Bill seemed distraught.

The older man shook his head and stepped over to one of the benches lining the wide walkway. Zack saw Tate pause two rows away and just watch. Zack shook his head at Tate and went to join Bill on the bench.

"If you need help, what's better than being on the prayer chain at church," Zack said, remembering his parents participating on the chain. He'd almost forgotten about that. *Help me here, please, Father God. I'm floundering in the dark. If it's Your will I learn what's wrong with her dad, guide me. Don't let me make a mess of this,* Zack prayed silently, hoping the Lord would give him the right words to say.

"Don't need everybody and his brother knowing my business," Bill grumbled.

"Seems like you need all the help you can get."

The moments ticked by. The day grew warmer. Tate leaned against a car and watched from the distance. Zack waited.

The older man sighed. "Maybe you're right. It's going to come out eventually," Bill said resignedly. "I'm having kidney trouble. I have to come here several times a week for dialysis. I'm on the waiting list for a transplant."

Zack was startled with the revelation. He'd never expected something like that. Marcie would be devastated. He wanted to be with her when she found out.

"Is there anything I can do?" he asked. "Be tested for a match or something?"

Bill looked at him. "You'd do that?"

"I've got two, from what I hear, a person only needs one."

Bill shook his head. "I don't know what to say. I never would have suspected—" He stopped, looked away.

"I'm sure I'm not the only one who would be tested," Zack said, thinking of all the people in Rocky Point who liked and respected Bill Winter. "How would I go about that?"

"I haven't a clue. We could ask my doctor."

"No time like the present," Zack said. He stood and motioned to Tate.

When the sheriff joined them, he nodded to Bill.

"He and I are going in to talk to someone. Can you head for the E.R. and be there for Sean?"

"Sure. Everything okay here?" Tate asked.

"Will be," Zack said.

When they entered the outpatients' lobby, Bill thanked Zack for not telling Tate the true situation.

"Hey, it's your call. But sooner or later Marcie has to know, and I'd think sooner would be better. She's going to worry herself sick."

"That's why I didn't want to say anything. I'm managing with the dialysis so far. Once I know about a transplant, I figured I'd tell her. There's a lot of hope once the transplant takes place. I'm all she has, you know. There's no other family, so I wanted to spare her as long as I could." His skin almost seemed to reflect his gray hair. His expression was a combination of determination and regret.

Zack winced. If he had not left ten years ago, Marcie would have other family—him and any children they might have had. And Joe and Jenny.

"Let's see what we need to do. I'll go with you if you like when you tell Marcie," Zack said.

As they waited to see Bill's doctor, Zack marveled at the working of the Lord. He'd even proposed following Bill, never suspecting he would end up here. Without having to resort to subterfuge, he'd still found out.

In less than an hour Bill and Zack were heading

for the E.R. The testing procedure for donor compatibility hadn't been necessary once the doctor found out Zack's blood type. It was not a match with Bill's. But both men were more informed now.

Sean's mother was sitting with her son when they entered the E.R. Tate sat in a chair next to them. He rose when he saw Zack.

"Everything okay?"

Zack shrugged. "Long story. I'm going to drive Bill back to Rocky Point. Thanks for waiting."

"No problem. Bill, good to see you."

Bill nodded. "You might as well know, everyone will soon. I have kidney failure. I'm on a waiting list for a donor."

"Oh, man, that's tough." He glanced at Zack.

"I already talked to the doctor." He held out a folder. "I've got a lot of info on the transplant scenario. Unfortunately, I'm not eligible for Bill."

"Marcie know?" Tate asked.

"Not yet, but soon," Zack said, drawing a deep breath. He ached for the shock and fear she'd experience.

Sean was watching. Zack turned to him and his mother.

"Thank you for calling me," Earline said. "Thank you for taking care of him."

He smiled. "Sorry for the injury."

She looked at her son. "It's a guy thing. At least

the doctors don't think the hand will suffer permanent damage."

"You okay?" he asked Sean.

"Yeah. Sixteen stitches, can't get it wet, have to check in at the clinic in a week." The hand was splinted and bandaged. While not bulky, it was wrapped in a way to prevent much use.

"Take the time off," Zack said.

"I can still come in, watch, if nothing else," Sean said.

His mother looked at Zack as if hoping he could read her mind. Maybe he could.

"When you feel like it. And I'll explain things to Marcie. I'm sure she'll hold the job for you."

"Thanks." The teenager looked as if he wanted to say more. A quick glance at his mother and he looked back to Zack. "No one except my mom's ever done so much for me. Thanks seem dumb, not enough."

Zack gripped his shoulder, the emotions spilling over. "Any time," he said, glad he'd been able to help in a meaningful way. More reasons coming home had been the right thing to do.

When Zack and Bill reached the Winters' home, Zack went in with the older man.

"I'll call Marcie," he said. "You want to lie down or something?"

"No, I'm okay. Something to eat or drink?"

"No, thanks," he said, amazed that Bill Winter was offering him anything—though he supposed his own offer had changed things with the man. Zack placed the call to Marcie.

"Hi," she answered. He relished the happiness in her tone and hated to be the one to change it.

"Can you come over to your dad's now?" he asked.

"What's wrong?" she said in a worried rush.

"We'll tell you when you get here. Drive carefully."

"That'll have her flying home," Bill said from his place on the sofa. "I doubt driving carefully will figure into it at all."

"Yeah, I'm not so good at delivering bad news."

"You mean in person," the older man said softly.

Zack sat in a chair near the sofa. What could he say in response? The man was right.

In less than five minutes Marcie came flying into the living room, stopping short when she saw both her father and Zack.

"No fireworks?" she asked. "Is this a peace conference?"

"Cupcake, come sit beside me," her dad said.

Zack saw the expression change in her face. "What's wrong?"

Bill explained in a concise manner, ending with, "I didn't want you to needlessly worry. I'm in the Lord's hands. Whatever happens, happens."

"Dad, we could have been praying for you all these months." She gripped his hand. "I don't want to lose you. Can I donate a kidney?"

Bill smiled and patted her hand. "We can see. Zack already offered, but isn't a match."

Marcie looked at Zack. "You offered a kidney?" She was stunned. There were bad feelings from her dad and Zack still offered. Her heart blossomed at his generosity.

He nodded. "Wasn't a match."

"Thank you. I'll be a match, won't I?" she looked back at her father.

"There's no telling. Zack got a bunch of literature from the doctor. Read up and then decide. There's no immediate rush."

"It's hard to take in. Why didn't you tell me?" Marcie asked.

"I didn't want you to worry."

Zack stood. "I'll take off."

Marcie rose, as well. "I'll walk you out."

Once on the front porch, with the door closed behind them, she reached out to Zack. He folded her into his arms, holding her close, just being there for her.

"Is he going to die?" she asked against his chest.

"Not if he gets a transplant. In the meantime, he's on dialysis. That's where he's been going. I don't know who was more surprised at the hospital, him or me. If Sean hadn't injured his hand, I wouldn't have been there. God works in mysterious ways."

She leaned back a little. "He does. How's Sean?"

Zack brought her up-to-date on the teenager. Brushing back her hair from her cheek, he smiled at her. "You'll be okay. Your faith will sustain you. And if you get that prayer chain going, I bet we'll see other miracles in play. Call me if you need me."

Marcie nodded, then stepped back. "Thank you, Zack. I know you have other things to be concerned with."

"Nothing that compares with this. You call me if you want to talk, you hear?"

She nodded, patted his arm and turned to reenter the house, but not before looking back with a new expression for him in her eyes.

Marcie paused a moment to catch her breath and offer a prayer to the Lord. *Help me know what to do, Father. This is so unexpected. I need my dad.*

She entered the living room.

"Now, don't go worrying, cupcake. I'm on dialysis and the waiting list."

"But, Dad, you didn't need to go through this alone."

"I didn't want you to worry, Marcie."

"So tell me everything and how I can find out if

I can be a donor. If not me, then maybe someone at the church."

He sighed. "I didn't want to burden anyone."

"Dad! Honestly, I'm scared to death, but so glad to know. With the Lord's help, we can manage this."

Marcie called the restaurant and told them she wouldn't be back that day, and asked if Tim could come in and make arrangements to cover for Sean until the teenager was fit again. Then she prepared a nice dinner of salads and sandwiches for her and her father. They ate on the patio behind the kitchen. And talked.

When she offered to stay the night, her father shook his head.

"This is one reason I didn't want people to know. I'm fine. I can live a completely normal life with the dialysis as long as I'm careful. I don't want people fussing over me. You get on home and tend to your life. I know you're here for me, and that means the world. Tomorrow you can see about the compatibility tests and we'll go from there."

"Okay. If you're sure." She hated to leave. What if something happened?

"Trust me and in the Lord," he said, giving her a hug. "Remember, this is my life, the path God has for me. You can join in on the journey, but it's not your path. God has a plan for each of us. Seek His

will in your life, and let me follow the way He's
leading me."

She nodded, finding comfort in remembering her
father was in perfect hands.

When she got home, she called Zack. She
couldn't forget the comfort she felt in his arms. The
feeling he really knew what she was going through
and could make it better. She wanted to hear his
voice.

"I'm so scared," she said.

"Would you like to come over here? We can tell
Joe and Gillian together."

Grateful, she managed a yes.

When she turned in the driveway of the old house
on the bluff, she felt relief. Her friends would rally
around. The entire town would, she had no doubts.
But for her it was so much more personal. Her dad!
What would she do if he died?

"Hey, honey." Gillian came out of the house and
reached out to hug Marcie as soon as she was out
of her car. "Tough times. Cling to the Lord."

"I am. And so's my dad." Marcie returned the
hug and then was swept up by Joe and then Jenny.

"We're praying for your daddy," Jenny said. "God
loves him, you know."

"I do know," Marcie said, giving the girl a hug.
Zack stepped into the circle and she felt as if she'd
come home. He gave her a hug, then with an arm
slung over her shoulder turned toward the house.

"Gillian made the most fantastic pineapple up-side-down cake. I saved you a piece," Zack said.

"I brought the info you got today," she said. "There's so much and some of it's confusing.

"We'll all read it together," Gillian said.

"And tomorrow I can be tested," Joe added.

"Probably won't match. I didn't." Zack urged Marcie into the family kitchen. In only moments, the adults sat around the table, hot coffee for each, and a large piece of cake in front of Marcie. Jenny hung around for a few minutes, then went to play in her room.

"Family conference," Joe commented.

"What?" Gillian asked.

"When our folks were alive, we'd have family conferences to discuss things pertaining to the entire family, such as where to go on vacation, what to donate to the church rummage or when Zack and I could have a car."

"I remember," Zack said, looking at Marcie.

"I'm not really family," she said.

"Yes, you are," Gillian spoke firmly. "I've learned family is more about love and commitment than blood ties. Besides, we're all joint heirs of the Father, so that makes us family."

Marcie couldn't help thinking of what life would have been like had she and Zack married. She would feel more like family with that tie. But Joe had relied on her when his first wife had died. She knew he and others in town would offer whatever support they could. She hadn't expected him to offer to donate. Nor Zack. There was more to the Kincaid men than met the eye.

For a moment she yearned for the closeness she and Zack had had when teenagers, for the feeling that one special person cared for her more than anything. Since he'd been back, she'd been tempted to give in to her need to recapture that feeling. Holding off for fear of being hurt again kept some distance between them. Would this crisis heal that breach or widen it?

What was she thinking? He'd already said he was going back to racing. He would be leaving in a couple of weeks or so. She'd known all along he wouldn't stay, despite his protestations. Maybe he saw himself staying, but she knew he'd grow restless and bored in Rocky Point. Time for her to pull back a little, so his departure would have less impact than last time. Surely she'd learned that lesson!

"Have you talked to Pastor John yet?" Gillian asked.

"Dad called him this afternoon. They're meeting in the morning. In the meantime, we've added his name to the prayer chain per Zack's suggestion."

Joe looked at him in surprise.

Zack shrugged. "It's what Trinity people do."

"And you remembered that after all these years?" Joe asked, looking surprised.

"I believe I've seen the power of prayer first-hand," Zack said.

"You have?" Marcie asked, startled.

"Jenny told me she and Joe have been praying for my safety and return home. Both requests answered. Can't go against stuff like that."

"And we'll be praying especially hard when you return to Europe," Joe said.

"And for you and your father," Gillian added. "In fact, let's open this meeting with a prayer. *Father God, we praise You for all Your mighty works. We are looking to You now, Father, for healing for Bill Winter and peace in his heart and in Marcie's. We thank You for keeping Zack safe all these years and rejoice he has returned home. Amen.*"

Everyone looked up and began to talk about what could be done for Bill. The literature was read and discussed. And after talking with her friends long enough to be buoyed up by their positive thinking, Marcie said it was time to return home.

"I'll drive you," Zack said.

"I drove here, I can drive home," she said.

"It's late. You've had an upsetting day. I'll drive you home, and bring your car to you tomorrow in time to go to work. What time is that?"

"Before seven. The weekends are hectic and I like an early start."

"Ouch. I guess I can get up that early," he said with a teasing grin.

"You better," Joe said, returning the smile. "I need you in the shop earlier than the banker's hours you've been keeping."

The drive to town didn't take long. When he stopped behind the bakery, Zack got out and opened the door for Marcie, escorting her up the stairs to her door.

"Thanks for everything, Zack. It's hard to know, but better than wondering. Now I wish his mysterious disappearance had been about a lady friend," she said.

"I know. But the Lord will see you through this."

"So are you getting back in touch with God?" Her eyes widened in surprise.

"I believe so. I've done a lot of thinking since I've been back. Talking to Jenny with her clear, strong faith, talking to you. I think maybe God didn't forsake me. I turned away."

"He's always there waiting for you," she said softly, her eyes shining with happiness.

"I know that, now. And He's always there for you." He tilted up her chin and brushed his lips lightly across hers. "I'm here for you, too, Marcie. Lean on me."

The lighting was dim, but she saw the sincerity in his gaze. She wanted to tell him she loved him, but now was not the time or place. In fact, it might be a burden for him to know that. He'd moved on, and she'd thought she had, but for a moment the yearning to be Zack's girl again was so strong she almost blurted it out.

"Good night," she said, and quickly went into the apartment, closing the door and leaning against it as she relived that faint kiss.

Chapter Nine

The next morning Zack and Joe sat in the kitchen of the family home finishing their coffee. *And* their conversation.

"You sure you want to do that?" Joe asked.

"I'm sure."

"You've prayed about it and all?"

"One thing coming home has done for me is reconnecting me to the Lord. I've been a bit rusty at the prayers, but I'm getting back into it. Yes, I prayed last night after I took Marcie home. I'm feeling pretty confident the Lord is moving me in this direction. You don't need the house. You'll be living in Gillian's. Unless you want to keep it for Jenny."

"Hey, I only own half. I don't expect her to live here. If you want to buy me out, fine, I'll put the money in a college fund for her."

"And any other kids you may have."

Slowly Joe smiled. "Yeah, and any others Gillian and I might be blessed with. She's going to be a fantastic mother."

"To you she's fantastic in every way."

"That, too," Joe acknowledged.

"I'll call Julian Green and set up an appointment," Zack said, glad to resolve the issue of home ownership. When their parents had died, they'd left their entire estate to their two sons, half and half. After Joe married Pamela, Zack sort of mentally relinquished his ownership, planning for them to live there forever. And now that Joe was marrying Gillian, if they hadn't had other plans, Zack would have been fine with his brother's living there.

But now, he wanted a place of his own. Where he could raise his own family and settle in. This place had a view of the sea. The only thing lacking was a white picket fence.

"I'm serious about buying into the business, if you'll let me. I need something that I can contribute to."

"What about the driving course?"

"That, too. Do you think I can't do both?"

"I think you can do all you want, if it's the path the Lord has for you." Joe studied his brother for a moment. "You're really going to stay? Maybe you should wait until after the next race. Once back on the track, you might change your mind."

Zack shrugged. "If you want to wait, I'm okay with that." He leaned closer, holding his brother's gaze. "But I'll be back right after that race." He wanted to pound the table in frustration. No one believed him about this.

"Besides, I have the defensive driving course to lay out. On the ride back from the hospital yesterday Bill Winter and I spoke about insurance for what I have planned. I'm talking to the owners of the mill today. There's a lot more involved than I originally thought, but I'm up to the challenge. I think it'll be something teens would like."

"What's not to like, driving fast in a safe environment, with instruction from a famous race driver."

"Fame is fleeting. In ten years no one will remember."

"Don't count on that, bro, you're Rocky Point's claim to fame. We have long memories."

"I know that! I wish people would forget how I left Marcie."

Joe nodded slowly. "I expect you do. That's a hard thing to forget. Especially when Marcie is so well liked. Actually, hard as it is to believe, folks liked you, too."

"You've been close to Marcie over the years. Do you think she'll ever get beyond it?" Zack asked.

"Why're you asking?"

Zack stared at his coffee for a moment, then raised his gaze back to Joe's. "I want her as my wife."

"Whoa, are you serious?"

Zack nodded. "I made a mistake, okay. Now I want to make it come right."

"That's a hard one. Up to Marcie, and I couldn't begin to guess how she might react."

"I think she's softening toward me. I mean, she came right here last night. Doesn't that count for something?"

"Sure it does," Joe said gently. He rose and carried his cup to the sink, looking over his shoulder. "Just go easy and make sure you deliver on any promises you make."

Zack knew he deserved that comment. He'd asked her to marry him before, which was a kind of promise to be there, to go through with the wedding, to build a life together. Instead...

"I'm taking Marcie's car back for her. She said she'd walk to work—do I park it there or at her apartment?" Zack asked as Joe prepared to leave for the shop.

"Apartment. She likes to walk to work in nice weather."

"You know that and I don't. I've got a long row to hoe," Zack mused.

"There was always something special between the two of you. If you're serious, I'd say do your best. If not, leave her alone. She has enough on her plate right now."

But he *was* serious. He just had to prove it to everyone.

On Monday morning, when Zack reached the shop, he was surprised to see Sean already there, hanging over one of the engines Joe was working on.

"How's the hand?" Zack asked when he joined them.

"Hurts, but I didn't want to take pills since I'll be around equipment," the teenager said.

"Take your pills, it'll help in the healing. And you won't get so woozy you can't function. You won't be operating the machinery," Zack said.

"I called Marcie yesterday and she said I can still work—at the cash register. My right hand works fine," Sean said, holding up his uninjured hand.

"Good deal. What have we here?" Zack asked, eyeing the engine.

Joe explained, mostly for Sean's benefit, and soon they were busy tearing the engine down and examining each part. The morning passed swiftly and the men working in the shop broke away from work around twelve-thirty for a lunch break.

"I'm heading home to clean up and get to work," Sean said.

Zack was wiping his hands with grease remover.

"Good idea. Later I'm talking to the mill owners about the driving course."

"Hey, man, that's cool. How soon do you think before we can start?"

"After I get back, most likely."

"Back from where?"

"He's got another race, in Stockholm in a couple of weeks," Joe said.

Sean's excitement faded. "Oh."

Zack picked up on it right away. "I'm coming back."

"Sure. See ya, I've got to get home." Sean left without another word.

"Actions speak louder than words," Zack quoted, tossing his towel on the bench.

"Meaning?" Joe asked.

"Once I've been here for fifty years, folks might believe me when I say I'm settling in Rocky Point."

"Yeah, maybe. Fifty years, huh?"

"I'm hoping for that much with Marcie. Maybe longer if the Lord wills it," Zack said.

Just then Marcie stepped into the garage, a sack in one arm and a tote hung over one shoulder. His expression lightened when he saw her. He would put aside anything and everything to spend time with her.

"Anyone hungry?" she called out.

The two mechanics who had been with Joe from

the beginning, Paul and Chas, looked up from the makeshift picnic table where they were eating. "Yeah, if it's some of your food," Paul called.

Marcie laughed and headed for the table, waving at Zack and Joe. "I've brought enough to feed an army, though it looks as if your wife packed you more than enough, Paul," she said. Setting the bag on the plank table, she started pulling out sandwiches, cookies and apples. A large thermos and a stack of plastic glasses soon appeared.

Zack and Joe joined the others at the table. "You staying?" Zack asked Marcie.

"I am. I wanted to thank you for yesterday. It means a lot. Plus, the first aerobics class starts at two. I'm making sure I'm not late."

Zack held her gaze. "You doing okay?"

"Yes. After I got home from your place, my best friend Jody called. She had just heard. It's good to have friends rally around."

He wanted to be considered more than a friend, but knew he had to take things slowly. And wait for better timing. Who wanted to be courted when worried about her father's very life?

Whoa, *courted*. That sounded old-fashioned and antiquated. Yet it was exactly what he wanted to do. Court this pretty woman who had too much to forgive.

Chas told Marcie he'd heard about her dad and

asked if there was anything he could do. She said there wasn't, but she appreciated his support.

"Pastor John visited Dad and rallied everyone in the church. I don't think he'll have to cook a meal for months. And his fishing buddies have planned a schedule to take him up to Portland for the dialysis each time, and stay with him to keep his spirits up," she told them.

"And testing?" Joe asked. "I called the clinic this morning. That new nurse said I can come by this afternoon. Apparently there were a couple of others already asking."

"We're blessed," she said, tears threatening.

"So are we with this feast. Want me to say grace?" Zack asked to ease the growing tension.

She blinked and nodded.

When they'd finished lunch, Zack offered to walk out with Marcie.

"I've got an appointment with Julian around two. I heard you gave Sean another task, to keep him employed."

"Tim, the manager at the café, and I discussed it. We've rearranged some assignments and we'll each be picking up some of the slack. Good help is hard to find and Sean's a hard worker."

Marcie waved to an elderly woman who was getting into a car across the street.

"Who is that? She looks familiar," Zack said.

"Maud Stevens. She's the matron of honor at Gillian's wedding."

Zack stared at Marcie in surprise. "You're kidding."

"Maud has been a great friend of Gillian's. She can tell her all the stories about the great-grandmother she never got to meet. So when Gillian was first planning the wedding, she insisted Maud stand up with her. I'm one of the bridesmaids—there are three of us."

"Remember, the best man escorts the matron of honor during the reception," Zack said.

"Yes."

"I thought I'd sit with you," he said.

Marcie nodded, her smile hard to hide. "I'd like that."

"You've been waiting for me to find out that I'm paired with a great-granny, haven't you?

She laughed. "I did wonder if you knew. Gillian's having a get-together next Saturday so everyone can contribute their suggestions for her wedding. Her mother's dead, so she doesn't have anyone to help her."

"Her father?"

"Oh, don't go there. He tried to swindle the house away from her. Anyway, no one knows where he is. But she has plenty of friends at Trinity. We're going to make sure it's the best wedding ever."

"We thought ours would be the best ever," he said gently.

The smile faded from her face. Zack could have kicked himself for bringing it up.

"I've got to get to class," Marcie said, turning to the building next to the garage. She scooted in the door, leaving Zack standing alone on the sidewalk.

"That went well," he murmured. *Lord, help me, please. I am stumbling and obviously need help in making things right. If that's what I'm supposed to be doing.* He had a few minutes before he was due at the attorney's, so Zack crossed the street and headed for Trinity Church. Entering a few minutes later, he was immediately enveloped with the sense of peace. He sat on the last row and bowed his head to pray a request for forgiveness.

Marcie returned to the café after the aerobics class, feeling calmer than she had in ages. The kitchen was quiet as the last of the lunch crowd had been served a while ago. She went to change into the waitress uniform she kept in her office. She'd be helping out the rest of today and for the next few weeks until Sean's hand healed. She admired the young man who wanted to keep working even though injured. He could have begged off.

She was glad of the physical workout at Gillian's. Last night she'd been so restless after talking with

Jody. She'd wanted to go back to her childhood home and reassure herself her dad was still there. But she hadn't. Finally, she'd picked up her Bible and read where it fell open, in first Peter—*cast all your cares on me.* Prayer had finally enabled her to find peace and sleep for the rest of the night.

Focus on the Lord, and on what He wants, and let God work in both her father's life and Zack's. She didn't even know when he was leaving.

And couldn't trust he'd return.

Instead of staying away, she'd deliberately put herself in his path today, taking lunch to Joe and the other men in the shop. She'd known Zack would be there. Why not just admit she was as fascinated by him now as before? Actually more so. She could see the man he'd become and for the most part admired him. No one said he had to do so much for a fatherless teenager. No one said he had to drop everything to return to help his brother. And no one said he had to be so kind to her own father yesterday, when Bill had been nothing but scathing since Zack had returned.

She wished she knew what to do. Afraid of being hurt closed her off. Was there a chance he meant what he said? Dare she step out in faith? It was so much easier to trust God. *If it is Your will Zack and I reconnect, Father, please let me know that. Fear is not what You want for my life. Show me Your way, please.*

Time to get to work. Putting on a bright smile, she headed for the customers.

By the end of the day, Marcie knew she'd sleep well that night. Everyone had something to say about her father's condition. Offers of help and support came from each Rocky Point customer she saw. Even some of the tourists apparently had picked up on the news and offered help. She was touched and amazed by the awesome power of God working through His children. She felt buoyed up and hopeful. And tired by the end of the shift.

She grabbed two dinners from the kitchen and headed for her dad's place. They ate on the patio, feeling the cool breeze that kept nights comfortable for sleeping.

"You have more friends than I knew," she said.

"Indeed. And I think everyone has called here today," he said. "Never been on the phone so much."

She grinned. "Good for them all. I heard about the escort service to the hospital."

"Yeah, didn't want to bother those guys, but they insisted. Walt's taking me tomorrow."

"I could take you."

"You have your work, he's retired. Besides, more fun to talk about fishing than watch you worry."

"I'm not worried. Your care is in the hands of God. I'm going with whatever He decides." She reached out her hand. "Just always remember I love you, Dad. If you go to your final home now, I'll be along after a while."

"Don't make it too soon, cupcake. Enjoy the life God has planned for you on earth. You might even consider taking up with that Zack Kincaid again. I saw the way he looked at you."

"Did you know he's heading back to Europe for another race?" she asked, startled with her father's about-face.

"No. When?"

"In a couple of weeks, I think. He might not come back." She wanted people to argue with her, to convince her Zack would return.

"Is that what he says? What about this driving course he bent my ear about yesterday?"

"Something to do, I guess. If he doesn't return, Sean's the only one who's going to be upset." And her. Again.

"Zack said he's not coming back?" her father asked for clarification.

She sighed softly and shook her head. "He insisted he'll be back. Then he got all huffy and said he wouldn't be telling me or anyone else that anymore. I'm not the only one with doubts."

"A man's word is his bond. If he says he'll be back, he'll return," her father said.

"Maybe." She couldn't help remembering he'd said he'd marry her and look what had happened. Which reminded her…

"We're having a prewedding party to sample the hors d'oeuvres I'm planning for the wedding on Saturday. Remember I did that with Kristin Jones's wedding? It'll give me a good idea of what's the best way to coordinate things and Gillian a chance to decide on the menu," she told her dad.

"You doing the cake, too?"

"Nope, Sunshine Bakery is doing that."

"Same as yours," her dad said.

Her smile was bittersweet. "Yes, only I don't think Joe's going to flit away. He's really in love with her—it's fun to see."

"Tell me what you're planning," he said.

The meal passed swiftly with Marcie talking about stuffed mushrooms, crab cakes and other delicacies Gillian wanted. Her dad looked tired, so Marcie got up to leave, admonishing her dad to get some rest.

When Marcie returned to her apartment, she had messages waiting on her answering machine. Listening to them, she was pleased to hear the offers of help from friends, including Gillian. Smiling, she called her back. After asking about her dad, Gillian brought up the sampling party.

"Should we have it at Joe's or at my place?" Gillian asked.

"Your call. Both kitchens offer lots of space for prep work."

"And the Cabot sisters won't mind working from my kitchen?"

"Theirs is probably just as old-fashioned. I thought you were going to get new appliances."

"One day. But I'm getting used to the old gas range. So, does Saturday still work? I know if something comes up with your dad, you might have to bow out."

"I think we'll be fine. The sisters are the best cooks and I'm letting them do most of the work. But I stuff the mushrooms."

Gillian laughed. "Did you see Zack today?"

"Yes, before class." Marcie went on alert. "Why?"

"I just wondered. If I weren't already totally in love with Joe, I think I'd find Zack an intriguing man."

"He can be," Marcie agreed. To change the subject she began speaking about Vacation Bible School and how much Jenny was looking forward to having Gillian teach their grade. She didn't want her friend painting the man in a favorable light. She needed to keep her distance, even when her heart yearned to talk to him, to hear his strong voice reassure her everything would be all right. To believe she could lean on him as he'd suggested.

She had no sooner hung up from talking with Gillian, than Zack called.

"How're you holding up?" he asked.

"Better than I would have thought. Dad's amazing. He's going along like everything's going to be fine."

"It probably is. Modern medicine can do wonders. I think his spirits are high, which goes a long way."

"I guess so."

"I just talked with Brett Spencer, remember him?" Zack asked.

"Sure, I see him occasionally. How's he doing?" Brett had been in high school with them. He'd gone on to college and worked in banking, as she remembered. He no longer lived in Rocky Point, but visited his parents often.

"Fine. I was surprised to hear from him, though we've kept in touch a bit over the years. He actually came to one of my races when I was in Italy about four years ago. The thing is, he invited me and you to go sailing with him. He has a new boat and apparently wants to show it off to everyone he knows."

"I can't go," was her first response.

"Why not? You don't even know when or where."

"With my father so sick, how can I take off and go sailing?" Besides, it would be more like a date with Zack and she had to stand firm in her resolve to stay away from him.

"I'm sure your dad doesn't want you to put your life on hold while he awaits a transplant."

She knew that Zack was totally right. But how could she say she couldn't go for the real reason—she was afraid to fall in love with him?

"It'll do you good and help you forget some of the worry about the situation," he said softly.

Indecision. She'd love to clear her mind and skim across the waves in a sailboat. She'd love to spend time with Zack, only—dare she waver?

"Come on, Marcie, it's just a couple of old friends visiting—on a sailboat. He invited us for next Saturday."

"I need to work on Gillian's reception menu."

"That tasting's not until the week after. You can spare a day. Say yes."

Oh, Father God, this is so hard. I do want to go. I'd love to feel carefree for one afternoon, forget all the things coming at me now. Should I go?

Zack didn't press her, as if he knew she would be praying about it. Finally, she decided to go.

"Okay. Should I pack lunch or something?" Her spirits rose. For this short time she was going to forget the situation and enjoy her afternoon with Zack and his friend.

"He said it's all taken care of. Bring your bathing suit—we might go swimming."

"I don't think so, that water's too cold for me."

"We used to love swimming at Carlisle Beach when we were younger."

"I remember, first we'd play in the surf and then

dry out on the warm sand. It was still cold!" She smiled at the memories. They were not hurtful, but bound the two of them together, memories of happier times.

"Suit yourself."

She *tsk*ed at his pun. "I'll wear shorts and let the rest of you hardy folks brave the water."

"Not me. I forgot how cold the Atlantic can be. Last time I went swimming it was in the Med."

"Umm." Of course it was. He had lived in Europe for years. His playground would be the Mediterranean Sea, with endless white sandy beaches and warm water, not the cold North Atlantic or the rocky shoreline of Maine. But he was here now, and she was going to do her best to enjoy every moment together!

"I'll pick you up at nine-thirty," Zack said.

"Wait, does Brett know we are not together?" He had to—hadn't he been invited to the canceled wedding? Then called to ask after her when it was off.

"I'm sure he knows."

"So, why invite you and me?"

"Maybe he's been seeing us together and assumes we've taken up where we left off."

"Which we're not." She had to be clear on that.

"See you Saturday," he responded.

Marcie wished he'd confirmed her assessment, but he had already hung up.

Just because circumstances put them together didn't mean they were falling in love again.

Except, Marcie didn't think it was *again*. She had always loved Zack. Actions spoke louder than words—why else could she not become interested in the other nice men who had asked her out? After a few dates, she always ended things, feeling it was unfair for them to develop feelings for her if she couldn't return them. She didn't want to feel this way. She wanted to move on with her life and not long for things that could never be.

Even if Zack fell back in love with her, would the same thing happen? Would they make plans to build a life together, only for him to be lured away by the excitement of living in Europe, racing the wind? Or was he truly back for good—after the next race? She wished she knew. Really knew.

She feared there would always be one more race.

Saturday Marcie was more than ready for a day sailing. All week the main topic of conversation around her centered on her dad. When she visited or spoke to him on the phone, he was calm and unworried. He urged her to try to ignore the situation, which was not getting any worse, and go on with life. Finally, exasperated, Bill told her that had been one reason he hadn't told anyone—he did not want people hovering over him.

Today Marcie was going to follow her dad's orders and stop hovering over him. She was taking today just for herself. She put on a sleeveless yellow top, denim shorts and deck shoes. Grabbing a sweatshirt in case it turned cool, she headed for the living room to wait for Zack. She slathered sunscreen on her arms and legs and face. She didn't want sunburn to mar the day.

It was almost nine-thirty. She went to the window overlooking the street to watch for him. For a moment she felt like she had in high school, anticipation building as she waited to see him again. And when she did, then and now, her heart would catch and her attention would focus solely on him.

When he got out of the truck, he looked up, as if anticipating she'd be watching.

This was just an outing. A friend of his had invited them. A break from the worries of the day. She took a breath and grabbed her sweatshirt. She would not read more into this than was warranted.

She started down the stairs just as Zack was starting up. He paused, watching her come down. She recognized the look in his eyes, the same one she had seen when she'd rushed out to meet him when they'd been dating in high school. Her heart kicked up another notch.

"Hi." Was that breathless voice hers?

"Hi, yourself. I see you're ready."

"It is a beautiful day and I'm looking forward to a sail."

He fell into step with her when she reached the pavement. In only moments they were in his truck and heading for the marina.

"When was the last time you went sailing?" he asked.

"Last summer. Betsey Isleton invited a bunch of us from church to go out on her sailboat. Jody and I and Betsey were best friends in school, remember?"

"I remember Betsey. Where does she live now?"

"New York. Long Island, actually. She's a graphic designer and loves working for an ad agency."

"Must be doing all right if she can afford a sailboat."

"She married a pediatrician. They have two little girls and this big beautiful sailboat. They were taking a trip along the coast and stopped off in Rocky Point for a few days to visit with her parents. We had a great time, but I think her husband was overwhelmed by all the chatter."

"Do you keep in touch with everyone from high school?" he asked.

"Well, most of our class still lives in Rocky Point, so I see them all the time."

And you now, too, she almost added.

They arrived at the marina and immediately spotted Brett's sailboat. It was moored in a visitor's slip.

It was sleek and elegant and larger than the rustic fishing boats berthed nearby. The only boats still in harbor were tourist boats. Those who made their living fishing had gone out in the early hours.

When they stepped aboard the boat, Brett greeted them both, introducing them to his date, Susan Galloway, his fiancée. In no time Brett backed out the boat using the engines and turned her toward the open sea. Once clear of the harbor, he cut the engine. "Now we raise the sails," Brett said. "Remember anything from when we were kids?"

"Hey, I'm not in my dotage yet," Zack said.

Sailing had been a sport shared by most of the high school student body when Zack had attended. There'd been P.E. classes devoted to sailing. In short order, with both Susan and Marcie pitching in, the sails filled with wind and the boat skimmed across the water, seeming to float on the surface. The sea sparkled in the sunlight, the breeze steady from the north.

"This is the fun part," Marcie said, delighting in the carefree spirit that took hold. She could forget everything except her love of sailing.

"Going against the wind is harder," Susan said, "but I think Brett loves the challenge."

"What's not to love?" he called back from the wheel. Zack stood beside him, braced against the movement of the boat, legs spread a bit, arms across his chest, watching ahead.

"The work, go this way, go that way," she teased.

"Tacking is a challenge, not work."

The two women laughed. Marcie stretched her legs out, hoping some of the warmth from the sun would dispel the coolness of the air as she relaxed on the bench. "If I had a boat, I'd try to get out every day," she said, tilting her face to the sun.

Zack turned to look behind them, his gaze going to Marcie. She looked like she was enjoying herself, her eyes closed, face to the sky, a slight smile on her lips. He could stare at her all day. Especially when she seemed more relaxed than he'd seen recently. *Father God, be with Marcie. Give her the strength she needs to face the situation with her father. And with me. Guide me, please. If I have a chance, please don't let me blow it.*

"So, tell me about what's going on in your world of racing," Brett invited.

Zack turned back to his friend. "I'm giving it up. One more race, then I'm calling it quits."

"Why? Hey, aren't you at the top of your game?"

Zack shrugged. He wasn't telling all and sundry exactly why. "It's time. I've had a great run, learned a lot, seen a lot. But I'm going to be thirty soon. Time to settle down, wouldn't you agree?"

Brett glanced behind him, then back at Zack. "You and Marcie?"

Zack looked at Marcie. She was too far away to hear their conversation. He looked at Brett and said, "I wish. It's taken this long to get her to consider going somewhere with me. And before you say anything, I know I left the wrong way. I regret it, I've apologized for it. I don't want to hear about it anymore."

"Hey, your life. But consequences come from actions we take."

"I'm hoping one day she'll forgive me enough to take a chance on me again," Zack said quietly, looking back at the most beautiful woman he knew.

"There's a lot to be said for finding the right one and making a life together," Brett said.

"So says the newly engaged man."

He grinned. "Right you are. You should try it."

"I did. And it was great. Only we were too young."

"And one of you had wanderlust. What's to say you won't go off again?"

Zack shrugged. "I've had that question more than once, too. Only time, I guess." And his own determination. He knew now what was important in life. Faith, love of the Lord, family and friends. And a great place to live didn't hurt.

Marcie was having a wonderful, relaxing time. She and Susan had been chatting in the sun, but now Susan stood with a gleam in her eyes. "Let's ask Brett to let us steer. He and Zack can handle the sails and we'll drive the boat." Susan went to stand beside Brett, squeezing in between the two men. He automatically brought her in closer with an arm around her shoulders and looked at her when she spoke.

Marcie couldn't hear but she could see. The love shining between them made her ache with envy. She wanted that. Wanted a special mate in her life who would love her till death. She wanted a family and home and love and everything she'd lost when Zack had left.

Refusing to look at him, even when she noticed he'd turned to look at her, she looked to her right, across the blue Atlantic and into the distance.

He ambled back the short distance to the bench and sat beside her. "Susan says you two want to drive the boat."

Marcie smiled. "So her terminology isn't quite correct. She communicates."

"True, and my guess is Brett would give her anything she wants."

Marcie nodded, still looking across the sea.

"Marcie?" His voice was low.

She turned to look at him.

"Will you ever forgive me? I am so sorry for the wrong I did. I would never hurt you like that again. Can you forgive me?"

"Oh, Zack." She reached out to touch his arm, her heart warmed by his sincerity. "I forgave you a long time ago. I didn't understand things, but I loved you. You didn't want to be married, I get that. I get that you were young and running to a dream I didn't even know about."

"I don't deserve it," he said.

She shrugged. "Forgiveness isn't about deserving, it's about forgiving. Letting go. Not dwelling on any wrong done."

"You've always had a generous heart," he said.

"No, it's a struggle. But I want to live my life as close to the Lord as I can."

He took her hand, holding it in his. "Does that forgiveness go as far as taking another chance for us?"

She was tempted to say yes. She wanted him to kiss her as he had when they'd been together before. Like he had the other night. She wanted what Brett and Susan had. What Joe and Gillian had. But fear of being hurt again, of being left behind again, rose up. Slowly she withdrew her hand.

"Let's just be friends for a while longer." *Until you leave,* she thought. Until you resume your life in Europe and forget about Rocky Point for another decade.

Chapter Ten

Zack was disappointed, no two ways about it. When she said she'd forgiven him, his heart rose. But it wasn't enough. He wanted more, though he should be grateful for what he had. Hadn't Saint Paul said he'd learned to be content in any situation?

He had his life, which was more than Jacques had. He had his family, expanding now with Gillian joining them. And he had forgiveness from the woman he'd wronged.

Patience. That's what he prayed for now. Patience to win Marcie's love back and a hope she'd say yes one day.

Brett and Susan had brought lunch—crab sandwiches, slaw and a chocolate cake that tasted delicious. They dropped the sails and let the boat drift as they ate, talking about the past and the future. Brett had heard about Marcie's father and expressed his concern. Zack told him about Joe's upcoming wedding. Marcie talked about her part in the wedding and how excited Jenny was. Susan talked a bit about her work as an investment consultant.

By the time the four of them returned to the marina, it was late afternoon.

"Care to come to the café? Dinner would be on me," Marcie invited.

"Another time, maybe. Mom has dinner for us today," Brett said. "It's been great to see you two again. I'll let you know the next time I'm in town."

"Zack probably won't be here, but I will," Marcie said.

He wanted to deny that, but it was true. Depending on how soon Brett returned, Zack could be back in Sweden for that last race. He'd had a call from Thomas before leaving this morning, urging him to return sooner rather than later. Plane tickets were waiting for him. The pressure grew to get to Stockholm in time to practice before the qualifying events. He'd been away from racing for several weeks, the longest break he'd taken since starting. He knew his reflexes were in top condition. He knew the course. He could ace this race. Even the thrill of anticipation had been growing at the thought of one more race.

Once behind him, he'd focus all his attention on the new driving course here in Rocky Point, working with Joe and convincing Marcie she should marry him.

"I'll take you up on the dinner offer," he said to her.

She looked at him in surprise. "Sure."

He'd caught her unaware. If she hadn't wanted him to eat with her, she shouldn't have invited them all.

Goodbyes were said, with thanks and promises to get together when Brett and Susan were in town again.

"There's still plenty of light, want to walk to the restaurant?" Zack asked.

"But your car is here."

"I can walk back to get it, it's not that far."

"Nothing in Rocky Point is far from anything else. Sure, I'd like the walk. I still feel strange being on land after balancing on the water all afternoon."

They started up Main Street. Marcie noticed a light in the apartment over Gillian's studio.

"Did Joe rent the apartment?" she asked, surprised to notice it.

"Yeah, to a nurse who moved here a little while ago. She works at the clinic. Faith something. Said having an aerobics class below her home didn't matter as she'd be at work all day, and might sign up for an evening class herself."

"Nice for Joe. With Gillian's studio, he's fully booked again."

"Want to go someplace else for dinner?"

"No, I want to check in at the café. I had my loyal staff working all day. I feel guilty taking off like this and having fun all day and leaving them to all the work."

"Did they complain?"

She laughed. Zack was struck by the melodious sound. He could listen to her laughter forever.

"No. In fact, Miss Prudence Cabot told me quite frankly she liked me not butting in."

"You?"

Marcie wrinkled her nose at him.

He slung his arm across her shoulders. "Did you enjoy your day?"

"I did."

"Me, too, Marcie. I enjoy every day you're in."

"Don't flirt with me, Zack Kincaid."

"Why not, isn't it fun? Besides, I'm serious." He drew her closer until they were walking in step along Main Street. Shops were closing. Tourists and residents wandered by, some looking at them, others caught up in their own world.

The café was crowded when they reached it. The hostess told Marcie she expected a table on the terrace to open soon, but there would be a wait.

"I can't complain—this is great business," she said. "We'll wait outside."

There were benches along the front of the building. Two other groups were seated on two of them. Marcie led the way to the one at the far end and sat.

"Tomorrow a thousand things await, but for now, I'm content."

"Me, too," Zack said, wishing he could capture the hour and hold on to it forever.

The next Saturday afternoon, just before members of the wedding party for Joe and Gillian began to arrive at the old house Gillian had inherited, Marcie and the Cabot sisters showed up. Zack and Joe helped unload all the food they'd brought from the two vehicles.

"I thought the tasting party was sort of small," Zack commented as he carried yet another box of savory treats inside to the kitchen.

"It is, but I think this is enough food to feed the reception," Joe said.

Moments later Gillian was hugging Prudence and Priscilla Cabot and asking if she could sample just a few things before the others.

"Not yet, missy," Prudence said, slapping her hand when she reached for a crab-stuffed mushroom. "It needs to be heated."

Gillian gave her another hug. "Thank you so much for doing all this. I'm thrilled. It's going to be a true wedding feast."

"Of course it is. Go on, now."

Maud Stevens and Caroline Evans arrived next. Gillian greeted them warmly, ushering them into the freshly painted living room. Zack and Joe had been alternating painting her house and theirs. Pretty soon both residences would be rejuvenated for the years ahead.

Tate arrived next, with Paul following behind.

"Glad you're having this wedding at the church. The yard already looks like a parking lot. If we had the wedding here, it'd be full," Zack murmured to his brother, his eyes on Marcie.

"Gillian wanted it at the church. I'm okay with anywhere," Joe said, looking around for his fiancée.

She was talking with the guests who had already arrived. In no time, all were in the living room talking, laughing and discussing the plans for the rehearsal and dinner and the wedding itself.

Jenny rushed in with a file folder and a big smile. "I like these dresses. Gillian said everyone gets to vote, even the guys, though I don't get why. They're not wearing the dresses," she said, looking around at everyone.

"I told you, they know what looks good on girls," Gillian said, with a smile at her soon-to-be daughter.

Jenny took the folder to each person, beginning with Maud. The elderly woman took her time studying each dress. "You did good, child. These dresses will span the generations. I like this one best," she said, handing Jenny one of the pictures.

Jenny carefully marked a check in the corner and then took the folder to Caroline. The others watched as each woman and then each man made their selection. Jenny then took the folder to Gillian. "I think most like the dark blue dress on top," she said.

"You're right. You and Marcie did a great job selecting dresses. This one it'll be. I hope none need fittings, but the lady at the dry cleaner's said she'd rush them through if alterations were needed."

Zack smiled at his niece, remembering some of the parties celebrating his and Marcie's engagement, and the plans for the wedding. Where would life have taken them if he'd manned up and married her back then? They could have a couple of kids by now. Would they be living in some small apartment over the bakery or one like the place Joe rented out? Or would going in with Joe back then have resulted in a comfortable lifestyle by now?

He'd bet Marcie wouldn't have chanced starting her restaurant. She'd have been too busy making their home and watching any babies they'd had.

For a moment Zack tried to imagine children, but he couldn't. He'd done pretty much what he'd wanted—seen a large portion of the world. Raced cars to the utmost. Knew people on three continents and had enough money in the bank to live comfortably the rest of his life even if he never worked again.

Blessings.

The thought came out of nowhere. Or was it God reminding him of all he'd received from the blessings of God?

Zack rose and went through the kitchen and out back. The chatter continued behind him and the farther he walked from the house, the quieter it sounded until he could hear the wind blowing and the sighing of the waves on the beach below the bluff.

He stood where he and Jenny had stood before, gazing out to the horizon. If the world were flat, could he have seen Europe? No, but he knew where it was. He'd have to close his flat in Paris. Sell his car. It would be too much to ship it back to the States. Let friends know where they could find him. He was closing a chapter of his life, but not shutting down. He gave a brief prayer of thanks to God.

"Are you okay?" Marcie asked behind him.

He turned and watched her walk toward him. She was so beautiful, inside and out. And she'd forgiven him. He smiled.

"I'm fine, just thinking."

"About our wedding?" she asked. When she reached him, he turned to look east.

"That and other things. Did you ever consider we

would not be where we are today if we had married so young?"

"Meaning?"

"I truly wonder how content I'd be if I'd gone from high school graduation to husband and father."

"We make our own contentment, I think. Seeing blessings instead of restrictions or roads not taken."

"True. But there is a time for every purpose under heaven. I handled things badly, we'll both agree to that. But in the end, I wouldn't be the man I am today if I hadn't lived the life I've lived. It wasn't always easy."

"I guess I never thought about that. You were far from home, family and friends. In countries where you didn't even speak the language. You must have wanted that more than anything to go so far from all the familiar."

He looked at her. "You wouldn't be who you are, either. If we'd married, would you have wanted a restaurant, made it the success it is today? Provided income for several families and a wonderful, honest place people can enjoy good food for reasonable prices?"

She was silent for a moment. "Probably not. I would have been content to keep house for us and then take care of any children we had."

"We would've had no money, not much in the skills department, not much hope of a great life if we'd married so young."

"Others do it."

"And there are scads of couples who don't make it."

She looked up at him. "Are you trying to convince me it was a good thing you left?"

"Not exactly. Maybe I'm trying to understand life more."

"Reconsidering returning to Rocky Point?"

"Not at all. I'm looking at it as if we have different stages in life. First we grow up and get educated. Then first job, maybe marriage. Then another stage, maybe a continuation of what we started, maybe an entirely new direction. There will be choices along the way. How do we ever know which choice will be best in the end? Or if any make that much difference?"

"By trusting in the Lord," she answered promptly.

"I'm doing my best now. I didn't always," he admitted.

Her eyes studied his for a moment. "No one always does, I don't believe. But we can try."

He reached out and drew her closer, hugging her gently. "I believe the Lord is leading me back to Rocky Point. And while I think I'm supposed to join Joe, I have a strong urge to do more with kids like Sean. Is that weird?"

"No, it's understandable," she said, encircling his waist and leaning against him slightly. Zack relished the closeness. It reminded him so much of what they'd had before.

"You lost your dad—you know what boys need. I think it would be a fine calling to mentor young men."

"Whoa, that's taking it too far. I just want a safe place for them to hang out and maybe get some driving skills that will be with them their entire lives."

"And provide a good role model in the meantime," she murmured.

"Marcie, would you marry me?"

She went perfectly still for a moment. Zack could feel his heart race. He had not meant to ask her so soon. He wanted her to become more comfortable with them as a couple. The words had slipped out, reflecting what he wanted more than anything on the earth.

She pulled away and shook her head.

"No, Zack, I can't do that. I can't. Not *won't*. It's just I'm not certain about anything—you, me, my father. You're going back to race. What if you get caught up in it again and leave? Better we just go on as friends."

She turned and hurried toward the house.

"I'm not going to get caught up in racing again. I'm coming back," he called. But the words did nothing to stop her flight.

"Way to go," he muttered angrily at himself.

He'd rushed things. But the thought of leaving her again was more and more difficult to deal with. He wanted some assurance she'd wait for him until he returned. And he'd blown it.

"Father God, what was I to do? I know You never give someone a dream without the means to achieve it. I dream of Marcie and me being together. I want to have the kind of relationship my brother and Gillian have. You know my heart, am I not capable of that? With You I can do all things— especially be a good husband to Marcie. But if that's not Your will, I stand ready to discover what is and follow," Zack prayed aloud, searching the sky as if answers would be written clearly for him. Only the clear blue of a cloudless sky met his gaze. Yet peace descended. He had made amends with his God and knew the future would be different from the past. He was not alone.

Marcie stopped in the kitchen, catching her breath. Her heart raced. Zack had asked her to marry him—again. She'd almost said yes. She'd wanted to, but then the memory of the day after he'd told her he was leaving flashed into mind. The heart-stopping numbness, incredible hurt. How could she risk her heart again? She had too much to deal with; she was not strong enough to manage another complication. Her father needed her. She had this wedding to contend with.

"You okay?" Prudence Cabot asked, looking up in surprise.

Marcie was afraid of what Prudence might speculate. She'd seen her follow after Zack when she'd told Marcie he'd gone out. Marcie nodded and headed toward the doorway.

Marriage. She was too afraid of having her trust shattered again to risk saying yes. He talked a good story, but as he'd said himself, only years of living in Rocky Point would show he meant what he said.

Yet for an instant she wondered if she'd made a huge mistake. She loved Zack. So what if he didn't stay—he'd come back, wouldn't he?

"Oh, there you are," Gillian said, peeping into the kitchen. "I wondered where you went."

"I just needed a minute," Marcie said with a smile, and went to join her friend.

"I can't believe how wonderful everyone is with this wedding," Gillian said as they walked back to the living room together. "You and Joe are so lucky to have grown up in one place. You have roots going back forever. And friends you've known since you were a baby."

Marcie nodded, struck by the fact that what she took for granted was really very special to someone like Gillian, who had moved so much as a child and had no family to depend on. Even if the worst happened to her father and he died soon, Marcie would have friends who were really extended family to be there with her, to remember her father and help with anything she needed.

"Soon you'll feel like you've known everyone forever, too. We are so happy you have come to live in Rocky Point," Marcie said.

The Cabot sisters came into the dining room bearing trays of goodies. In no time the wedding party was sampling tasty canapés, savory tidbits and fruit tarts. The sisters had even procured a small replica of a wedding cake from the bakery.

"I want that," Jenny said, pointing to the cake when it was brought in.

"Later," her father said with a smile.

There was plenty of food and everyone tried every dish, some more than once. Marcie was pleased with the menu and the efforts of the sisters. She insisted they join them to hear the compliments that flowed every time someone bit into a new treat.

Zack slipped in during the midst of the tasting and stayed away from Marcie, talking with Tate and Paul and keeping his gaze mostly on his plate.

Marcie felt extremely self-conscious and wanted to leave. But she would not do anything to detract from Gillian and Joe's happiness.

Once the food had been declared a total success, the group drifted back into the living room, where Gillian went over the plans for the rehearsal dinner—a barbecue at her home—and then the wedding itself.

When she announced Maud as her matron of honor, Marcie looked at Zack. His gaze flicked to her and for a moment locked on hers. If was as if he spoke his wish for her to have been his partner for the event. Then he smiled at Maud. "You'll look beautiful in the dress they chose," he said. "Though I'm a bit tall for you."

"I'll be just fine, boy. You watch me dance you under the table! Sophie would be so happy knowing her great-granddaughter will be living in her house."

"Are you sure you should be dancing?" her friend Caroline asked. "You're still recovering from a broken hip."

"Fiddle, that's fine as can be. This is my last chance to be a matron of honor, I'm going to have a ball!" the old woman said with fervor.

Everyone laughed with Maud.

Marcie wondered if she herself would be as feisty when she was ninety-three—or even if she'd live that long. For a moment she felt sad. Maud and her husband had been happy together. But he was gone and Maud had no children. Would that be Marcie's fate? All the more reason to stay friends with Joe and Gillian and claim Jenny as honorary niece.

The phone rang and for a moment the party grew less noisy when Jenny ran to answer it in the kitchen. She came back a moment later. "Uncle Zack it's for you, that man who keeps calling about your race," she announced.

Marcie looked at Zack and then away as he rose, excused himself and went to the kitchen.

He said nothing about the call when he returned. Once they'd finished discussing the wedding, people began to leave. Marcie went into the kitchen to help the Cabot sisters, trying to put the call out of her mind.

Prudence had wrapped the little food remaining and was stowing it in the refrigerator for the Kincaids to enjoy later. Priscilla had washed all the dishes and was drying them. Marcie pick out a clean towel and helped.

"Thank you both. Every selection was delicious," she said as they worked harmoniously together.

"Zack's leaving," Prudence said.

"I know."

"This week, from what we heard. He took his call here and we couldn't help but hear his end of it."

Marcie shrugged. "He's told everyone he's going back for a race. It's not a surprise."

Prudence and Priscilla looked at her with concern. "How do you feel about that?"

"I'm not surprised." She couldn't say any more. Not without thinking about his unexpected proposal a short while ago. How could he ask her when he knew he was leaving soon? He'd made no mention of that on the bluff.

"Wonder what Sean's going to do," Priscilla said.

"About what? He still has his job with me," Marcie said. "And hangs out at Joe's garage, which I don't see changing. Joe'll be good for him."

"He's set some store about Zack's promise of a driving track."

"We'll just have to see how that pans out," Marcie said, glad to have their attention on Sean and the track and no longer on her reaction to Zack's leaving. If she could just get to her home without breaking down, she'd be fine. The heartache seemed to grow when she thought she might not see him again for months or years. Had she turned him down too quickly? Should she consider all the ways a long-distance marriage between them could work?

"Do you need anything carried out?" Zack asked, coming into the kitchen.

"Just these pans and trays," Priscilla said, pointing to a stack on the table.

"I'll carry them for you," he said, glancing at Marcie.

Marcie went to tell Gillian and Joe goodbye. She tried to stay as far from Zack as she could. Once in her car, she felt she could relax—except for the echo of his urgent voice asking her to marry him. Was it just being around an engaged couple who was so happy planning their wedding that had prompted the proposal? She wished she were planning a wedding to Zack. Was it too late?

Marcie went to the restaurant, following the Cabot sisters. They unloaded the vehicles and then bid each other good-night. Once home, Marcie tried to quell her doubts, but the longing for Zack had her questioning everything.

She gave in to impulse and called him.

Joe answered and called his brother to the phone.

"Forget something?" Zack asked when he answered.

"No. Not that I know of. I, um, heard you were leaving sooner than planned and didn't know if we'd get to say goodbye this time."

"I'm leaving Friday. I would make sure I told you goodbye."

"Oh."

"And I'm coming back, Marcie. As I told you."

"Umm."

"This is getting us nowhere. Where's your faith?"

"In Christ," she responded instantly.

"In us?" he asked.

"There is no us. When were you going to tell me you're leaving earlier than originally planned? If I'd accepted your proposal would you have told me then?"

"I'd have asked you to go with me," he said. "It's

only one race. I'd like to have you see me race once. Especially if I win, which I usually do these days."

It was a world she neither knew nor understood. "I think I'd have been too afraid to enjoy it."

"Afraid of what?"

"That you'd end up like your friend. It doesn't seem worth it to drive cars in circles and end up dead."

"There's more to it than that. But Jacques's death was hard to take. And I don't plan to end up like he did."

"You don't know what the future holds."

There was silence on the line. "I don't, but I'm praying about it. Maybe I'll get an answer from the Lord. Until then, I'm putting one foot in front of the other until I get wherever I'm supposed to be on this life's journey."

"And you don't think that's racing anymore?" she asked.

"I'm not sure it ever was. I've been fortunate— blessed, really—though I don't deserve it. I was selfish ten years ago. With age has come some wisdom, I hope. And being back in Rocky Point gives me a connection that was missing. Life can be exciting and full and still empty if I'm empty inside. I'm not any longer, thanks to the Lord."

Pleased he was rediscovering his faith in God, she wished she could step out in faith to trust he meant what he said. That he would be in Rocky Point for the rest of his life. But the memory of her broken heart, the shattered trust, was hard to overcome.

"Help my unbelief," she said softly.

"A quote from the Bible?"

"And a prayer. Do say goodbye before you leave."

"And hello when I return."

"Sure." If you return. She didn't say the thought aloud but it echoed in the silence nonetheless.

"Good night, Marcie. I wish you'd said yes."

Chapter Eleven

The next morning, Marcie was nowhere near convinced she'd done the right thing in turning Zack down. Yet she couldn't go through what she had before—thinking they were building a life together and finding out that wasn't what he wanted.

Other people had long-distance marriages. And it worked for them. But she couldn't envision it.

Getting ready for church gave her time to put things in perspective. She was young, healthy, had a good business and many friends. She had the love of her heavenly Father and her own earthly father. And just maybe the love of a man she adored.

She headed out for church, still unsure, but trying to see what God held in store for her.

Gillian met her as they were walking to the classrooms and raved again about the food.

"You said you liked it yesterday," Marcie reminded her, pleased her selections had delighted her client.

"I know, but in munching on some of the leftovers this morning, I realized again what a wonderful selection everything is. Each piece is distinctive, yet they all go together. And the cake's delicious."

Marcie smiled. Sunshine Bakery's specialty was cakes, and all the cakes they offered were popular.

"You and Zack talk?" Gillian asked.

Marcie went on alert. What had Zack told Joe and Gillian?

"A little, why?"

"He seems really down today. Just wondering. I went over to fix breakfast before heading for church and he hardly said a word to any of us."

"Did he say when he was leaving?" Marcie asked.

"Yes, on Friday. But he plans to be back no later than three or four weeks after that. He's putting his Paris flat on the market."

"Umm."

"What does that mean?" Gillian stopped before they entered the classroom. Others in the Bible study greeted them and slipped past to enter the room.

"Don't you think once he's back in the swing of things he'll be caught up in that lifestyle again?" Marcie said when they were alone in the hallway again.

"Nope."

"Really?" Marcie was startled Gillian didn't see it her way.

"Really. He says he's coming back. He's put a lot of effort into, er, ah, different things. I believe he's coming back."

"What things?" Marcie asked.

"You know, the driving track. I believe he's serious about setting up something teenagers can do safely, to let off some steam. He's really caught up with Sean and concerned the boy has a strong male role model since his own father seems to have deserted the family."

"I don't see Zack as a father figure," Marcie said slowly.

"You've seen him with Jenny. He's a natural. I bet he wants a bunch."

Marcie remembered him at the picnic, caught by his own offer of help, surrounded by little girls who had a marvelous time playing throw-the-stick. Then the hero worship Sean showed anytime Zack's name was mentioned. And she did know Zack was pursuing the driving course. Would it be something left behind or was he really serious about returning?

He had never lied to her.

The thought struck her suddenly.

Marcie sat in the back of the room and started listening to the leader. But her thoughts drifted.

Zack had never lied. He'd skipped out on their wedding, but had called her to tell her, not left her to show up and find him gone. He'd been honest with her then. And now?

She'd thought she'd known him then. Now he was a mystery to her. After years apart, years doing things the other hadn't known about, they were like strangers—yet not. The common heritage of their childhood and teenage years bound them together. They'd grown apart during the last decade. Could they find the love that had once been theirs?

Marcie knew she loved Zack Kincaid. She always had. A binding, enduring love that would last all her life. Maybe tucked away these last years, but never extinguished. She couldn't deny the truth. She loved Zack.

She waited until Tuesday to call him. But she missed him. He'd gone to Portland on some errand Joe didn't know about.

Wednesday Marcie was too busy with a minor crisis in the kitchen to call until late afternoon, leaving a message when he wasn't there. Later she had a message from him, but she'd missed his call. She called again. Again he called when she was away from her phone. At the rate they were going, they would never connect.

Thursday Marcie panicked. Time was running

out. He was leaving in the morning. She wanted to talk to Zack. She needed to. She'd left messages, he'd left messages. She was about to glue her phone to her hand to be there when he called back. She kept missing him. She didn't want to be too late. She needed to talk to him. To see if they could possibly have a chance to work something out.

Still uncertain and a bit fearful, Marcie wanted to tell Zack she'd changed her mind. If his offer was still open, she would be happy to marry him.

She could step out in faith that what he said was true. He was coming back.

Now she hoped she wasn't too late.

When she called the shop a second time on Thursday, Joe answered.

"He's not here, Marcie. He's back at the house. He had something to wrap up before he leaves tomorrow. Want to call him there?"

"Sure. Just how much is he contributing to the partnership if he's never there?" she asked, frustrated to have missed him again.

"Ah, that partnership is on hold, actually," Joe said.

That made sense, since he was leaving. "I'll try him at the house." She hung up and thought for a moment. Phone calls weren't making it. She was going to go up there and talk to him face-to-face. Grabbing her purse, she called out to the kitchen staff as she left, telling them where she was going, not sure when she'd be back.

She wasn't going to dwell on Joe's comment about the partnership being on hold. That was between Zack and Joe. She was concentrating on the relationship between her and Zack. And hoping there was still one there to dwell on.

Turning at the driveway, she slammed on her brakes when she saw the new fence surrounding three sides of the house. The back was still open to the bluff and the Atlantic, but the rest was encased in a brand-new picket fence. She saw Zack midway up one side, painting it white.

For the longest moment she sat where she'd stopped the car, trying to figure out what Zack was doing painting a fence. Why was there a fence to begin with? It had not been there when they'd had the tasting last week.

Getting out, she walked over. He glanced up and then returned to painting.

"Hi," Marcie said, wiping her palms against her skirt.

"Hi." Zack dipped the brush in the gallon of paint and applied it to a picket.

"Nice fence."

He stopped a minute and looked down the length. "I think so."

"You put it up?"

"Had it installed."

She looked at Gillian's house, across an expanse of ground, clearly visible.

"I thought Joe and Jenny were moving in with Gillian after the wedding."

"That's the plan."

She looked at him, her heart swelling in love. "So, why the new fence?"

He looked at the brush, dipped it into the paint again.

"I wanted a house by the sea with a white picket fence," he said slowly.

Marcie was stunned. It was just what they'd talked about when they'd been engaged. What she'd always wanted, a house by the sea with a white picket fence. She looked at the Kincaid home, strong and sturdy. It had been in their family since Zack had been a boy.

"You planning on moving in?" she asked, her heart racing.

"Depends," he said.

"On?"

He stood up and held the dripping brush away from their clothes. "Why are you here, Marcie?"

"I've been calling you all week—you got my messages."

He nodded. "I was planning to tell you goodbye

before I left, but didn't see an urgent need to talk before that."

"Well, that's the thing. I do." She wiped her palms against her skirt again. He wasn't making this easy.

"About?"

"Us."

He looked at her and then at the brush. Stooping again, he applied more paint on another wooden picket.

"Past, present or future?" he asked after a moment.

"Future. And present, I guess," she said.

Her cell sounded.

She ignored it. It would go to voice mail. This was too important.

"Present we're here," he said.

"You're leaving in the morning, but will be back, right?"

He looked at her, his dark eyes narrowed slightly. "So I've said."

"I believe you."

"Since when?'

"Since I realized you've never lied once in your life. If you say you're coming back, I believe you," she repeated.

"What else do you believe?" he asked, putting down the brush and standing, stepping next to her, his arms crossed over his chest, his eyes locked with hers.

Her phone sounded again. She frowned and glanced at the caller ID on her phone.

"It's the clinic. Oh, no, Dad." She quickly answered the phone.

"Marcie? It's Faith Stewart at the clinic. I'm the new nurse here. Your father's being taken by ambulance to the hospital in Portland. He asked if I'd call you to let you know."

"What happened? When?" Suddenly she felt Zack's strong hand on her shoulder.

"He was in an accident and his arm was broken in two places—more complex than the doctor wanted to deal with here. Your father said don't rush, get to the hospital safely. But he will need transportation home."

"Thanks, I'll leave right now."

"What happened?" Zack asked as soon as she hung up.

"My dad's being taken to the hospital. He was in an accident. I've got to go."

"Hold on. I'll drive you."

"You don't need to, he's going to Portland. The nurse said it was a broken arm, but more complicated than they wanted to deal with at the clinic. I can get there okay."

"I know, but let me drive, Marcie," Zack said

calmly as he pounded the lid on the paint can and scooped up the brush. "I'll put these away and we'll go."

She nodded, worried about her father. She'd planned to visit him that evening. Now this. What had happened? How had he broken his arm?

In less than five minutes, Zack had them both in his truck and was turning the key. "How about a prayer before we go?" he said, reaching out to clasp her hand.

"I've been praying since I heard the nurse."

"Let's offer one together." He bowed his head and prayed for a safe journey, wisdom for the doctors at the hospital and strengthened faith for both of them to trust God and know that whatever the outcome, it was His will.

Marcie blinked when she opened her eyes. "That was nice," she said.

"Now let's get to Portland."

The drive seemed endless. Zack used all his skill to push the truck to the limit—of its abilities and the posted speeds. He did not want to endanger his passenger by taking unnecessary chances, but as the traffic grew heavier close to Portland, he did what he could to get Marcie there as quickly as possible.

He dropped her off at the E.R. and went to park the truck. Walking back to the hospital a couple of minutes later, he offered another prayer. *Keep her spirits up, please, Lord. And show me what I can do to be there for her and her father. We all need Your strength at this time, Father. Please be with us now, let Marcie feel Your love and find peace.*

Marcie was sitting along the far wall, looking tired, scared and small in the busy waiting room. He crossed over and took the chair next to her.

"Any word?" he asked, reaching out to take her hand in his. It was cold and small. He rubbed gently to warm her.

"He's in X-ray. Once he's back the nurse said I could join him. I can't imagine how he fell and broke an arm."

Zack looked around and to his surprise saw Tate walking in. The sheriff went straight to the desk, then turned and spotted Zack and Marcie. He walked over.

"Sorry about your dad, Marcie. He'll be okay, right?"

"I guess. Do you know what happened?"

"It was a hit-and-run accident. He was crossing the street and a car came through too fast. I need to talk to your father to get the particulars. Some of the folks on the sidewalk told me what they saw. He wasn't hit straight on, but it knocked him to the curb and I heard he broke his arm in two places."

"The nurse didn't tell me that," Marcie exclaimed. "Can you find the driver?"

"Already working on it. Sean was heading toward

your café and had the presence of mind to get the license number. As soon as we get the information, we'll find him. I wanted to check on your father and see if he can tell me any more."

They waited together until one of the nurses on duty came to Tate. Verifying he was there to see Bill Winter, she said, "The patient can talk to you now. We gave him some pain meds but he's lucid. Might go to sleep in a short while, though."

"I'm his daughter, can I see him?" Marcie asked.

The nurse nodded. "He's in cubicle three." She smiled and left.

Once crowded in the small cubicle, Zack stood near the curtain, not needing to be right there with Bill, but nearby in case Marcie needed him.

"I probably can go home after they set the arm," he said after Marcie had hugged him and exclaimed he should have called her right away. "I'll need a ride—don't want to take that ambulance again."

"Might be tight, but the truck has a bench seat. We'll take you back," Zack said.

Tate asked him questions about the accident, jotting notes and growing angrier by the moment. "Totally senseless. Thank the Lord you weren't injured any more than you were."

"I must admit I didn't see him coming or I wouldn't have stepped off the sidewalk."

"According to witnesses, he came around the

corner without stopping. Does the doctor say you're going to be okay?" Tate asked.

"I'll need to take it easy. Which I've been doing for months," Bill grumbled. "And probably no fishing until the cast comes off."

His cell phone rang.

"Uh-oh, no phones in the hospital," he said and pointed to his jacket pocket. Marcie reached in to pull it out. Glancing at the caller ID she frowned. "It's Betty, Dad's secretary. Did she know you were coming here?"

"Not unless someone told her." With a glance at the closed curtain, Bill flipped the phone open. "What?" he said a moment later. "You're kidding! Sure, I'll get in touch immediately. Thanks."

He looked at Marcie. "They have a kidney. It's on its way from New Orleans. I hope this broken arm doesn't delay anything. I might have the transplant today. I need to contact the doctor and let him know I'm already here. Betty said they were calling all over Rocky Point to locate me. And trying my cell every few minutes. Must have been ringing while I was in X-ray."

Just then a busy E.R. doctor hurried in, holding X-ray film in his hands. "So, Mr. Winter, we have what we need."

"I've just learned they have a kidney for me. I need to get in touch with Dr. Billings right away."

The doctor looked nonplused for a moment, then nodded. "Right away."

Zack and Tate stepped out of the cubicle, letting Marcie and her father have some private time while the E.R. doctor contacted Dr. Billings.

"Guess I'll head on back," Tate said. "I have what I came for. I'll let Pastor John and others know about Bill. We'll put him on the prayer chain."

Zack nodded, glancing at his watch.

"Problem?" Tate asked.

"No. I'll wait with Marcie."

"It could be a while, depending on delivery time of the organ."

"I'll wait." Zack wasn't leaving her to face this alone.

"I thought you were heading back to Europe tomorrow," Tate said.

"I didn't expect this. They'll have to do without me."

"Won't that hurt your racing team?"

Zack shrugged. "I told them before I was quitting. I'm sorry to cut out at the last minute, but there're two weeks before the race, time enough to get someone else who's dying for a shot. I've had a great run, but there are things more important, and I've just come to realize it. I'm not leaving until I know everything is going to be okay." And that Marcie no longer needed him with her. If that ever happened. He hoped it wouldn't.

"Man, you have it bad for her," Tate said with a grin.

"I always have. Things just got in the way, muddied up the water. I think I'm on the path God wanted for me now."

"Glad to have you back," Tate said, gripping Zack's hand and slapping him on the shoulder. "I'll let Joe and Gillian know, too."

"Yeah. In the meantime, I need to make a few phone calls."

Marcie sat beside her father, holding his hand, talking softly while the bone was being set and plaster applied. "I think it's a blessing there's a kidney for you so quickly."

"You're right. The chances weren't that great. The Lord is watching out for me."

"I'm so grateful."

"Now, Marcie, remember, nothing's guaranteed. This operation is tricky. It's going to take a while. You need to call Jody or Gillian or another friend to come be with you. And take time to rest. Don't hang around while I'm out of it, okay?"

"Dad, I'm not going anywhere. But I might call someone to come up. I'll need a ride home, at least, when the situation's stable."

"How'd you get here?"

"Zack drove me."

"He can't drive you back?"

"He's leaving in the morning for Europe. There

are lots of folks in Rocky Point who'll come, don't worry about that."

Bill frowned. "Don't let him hurt you again, cupcake."

"I don't think he will. He asked me to marry him again. I said no, but now think I should say yes. I still love him. I think it's the forever kind of love, so years and distance haven't and won't change it. Might as well give in and take what I can get when I can get it. Eventually he'll give up racing."

"Marriage isn't easy. A distant relationship would put added strain on it."

"Did you know when we were kids we used to imagine where we'd live? I always wanted a house by the sea with a white picket fence. When I drove over to see him today, before I got the call about the accident, there was a new picket fence around his family home and Zack was painting it white."

Her dad studied her for a moment. "He's doing it for you, trying to make some dreams come true," he said gruffly.

She nodded with a smile. "I think so, too. I'm trusting in the Lord this time around. We'll just see what happens, won't we?"

As soon as the cast was set, the E.R. doctor told Bill he would be going up to the surgery ward and prepping for the surgery, which would probably take place in the evening as soon as the kidney arrived. Marcie would be told where her father was and when she could see him again once they had him set up in the surgery ward.

She wandered out into the waiting room. No sign of Zack or Tate. Not that she expected either to still be there. Tate had said he'd let the pastor know. And Zack—he probably had some last-minute packing to do. She felt totally keyed up, worried about her dad's operation. It was a blessing they hadn't had much notice—she would worry herself sick if she had.

Walking out into the sunshine, she went to a quiet area near the entrance where there was a bench and a clay pot of cascading flowers. She sat and closed her eyes, praying for the Lord to give the doctor wisdom and keep her father safe.

"You okay?" Zack said.

She opened her eyes in surprise to see him there and nodded, feeling at peace. "Just praying."

He sat beside her and reached for her hand. "Let's pray together."

Her heart warmed at his renewed faith.

When they'd finished, she squeezed his hand. "Thanks for bringing me here." Dare she bring up his proposal?

"Of course I would. If I hadn't, I'd have come the minute I heard. What's going on with your dad now?"

"They're taking him for pre-op work and getting him a place in the surgery prep area. Then I can stay with him until time for the operation. I don't know when the kidney will arrive, so don't know how long it'll be until the operation. He's strong. He'll be okay," she said, trying to be as confident as her words.

"Whatever happens, I'll be with you," Zack said. "Your dad's still relatively young, he should come through with flying colors."

"I know you have to leave for Europe."

"Nope, cancelled."

"What?" She stared at him in stunned surprise. "Why?"

He raised an eyebrow. "You didn't think I'd leave just when you need me the most, did you?"

She bit her lip. She had thought he'd go. Vainly, she tried a nonchalant shrug, but tears flooded her eyes. "Thank you," she whispered, afraid her voice would crack if she spoke.

"Hey, I let you down before. History is not going to repeat itself."

"I'd understand this time. You have a commitment."

"My commitment to you tops any other in the world—except my commitment to the Lord. I could no more leave you now than I could cut off my right arm. I want to spend the next however long it takes for you to trust me again. And think of my proposal."

"I have been thinking about it."

"Shh, no talking about that now. We need to focus on your dad. We'll see him through this and then talk about us."

She nodded. "Just know I love you, Zack."

"Oh, sugar, I love you, too."

He kissed her and then rose. "Time to see to your father."

The surgery waiting room was more comfortable than the E.R. Marcie checked on her father and found he was already being prepped for surgery. The surgeon would begin taking his kidneys out and be ready to implant the new one when it arrived. It was due shortly.

"Let's get something to eat," Zack suggested.

"I'm not sure I can eat anything."

He took charge and in only a few moments they were selecting things from the cafeteria's menu. Sitting near a window, Zack watched her closely, as she seemed to be in a world of her own. His phone rang. It was Thomas. He'd called every half hour since Zack had told him he wasn't returning.

"Aren't you going to answer that?" she asked.

"No. Cell phones aren't supposed to be used in hospitals." He switched it off.

"Was that your manager?"

"Ex-manager."

"Whoa—what happened?"

"That's what he said if I didn't show up."

"Zack, they're counting on you. You have to go."

"Actually, I don't. I told them in May that I was through. The other driver sprained his ankle and can't race in Stockholm, so as a favor I said I'd fill in. But not now. You're too important to me, Marcie. We need to make sure your father's on the road to recovery before I consider doing anything but being with you."

"That's sweet, but I'll be okay."

"I know you will. I will be, too. But we'll do it together. When we finish eating, we'll go outside and call home," Zack said, "update everyone. Tate said he'd get the prayer chain going."

"Okay." She couldn't believe Zack was so attentive. It was like before—they each relied on the other, knew the other would have their back. She was so grateful he'd returned home. She nibbled at the sandwich she'd chosen. Not really hungry but not knowing when she'd eat again, she forced it down.

Later, calls taken care of, they returned to the surgery waiting area and were updated. Bill Winter was in surgery—the donated kidney had arrived. It was just a question of time now.

Hours passed. Zack seemed perfectly content to sit beside her. She wanted to jump out of her skin she was so worried about her father. Prayer offered an outlet. Then she rose and paced to the window, gazed outside wondering what life would be like if her dad didn't make it. Zack joined her, his hands on her shoulders, rubbing gently to ease the tension.

Leaning down a bit to put his face next to hers, he spoke softly, so no one but she could hear him.

"I love you, Marcie. I've always loved you. I want you to know you can rely on me to stand by you no matter what this time. I'm not taking off, unless you go with me. The entire Stockholm thing was a dumb idea. How can you trust me when you think I'll take off at a moment's notice?"

She turned slowly, staring into his dark eyes, seeing the sincerity. Fear for her father fled. She felt such an overwhelming love for this man who had once hurt her so badly. Truly forgiveness worked.

"I love you, Zack, I will always love you. I can't tell you how much I appreciate your being here with me today."

"Today and always," he said.

"I'd really like that."

He glanced around. "The time and place sucks."

She giggled. "Love is perfect anywhere."

He took her hand and walked to the nurses' station. "Can you take my phone number and call when there's news? We want to go outside for a bit."

In seconds he and Marcie were out on the grounds

of the hospital. Zack walked around the side of the building, looking for some private spot. If he didn't kiss her soon, he was going to explode. She almost ran to keep up with him.

"Where are we going?" she asked, tugging on his hand.

"Here's good," he said, pulling her into his arms near a large bush that would partially shield them from anyone walking on the grounds. He kissed her, hoping to convey all the love in his heart to the woman he adored.

It was easier to wait the long hours with Zack, Marcie realized as the afternoon faded into evening. She prayed her father would be spared for a while longer. But if not, then she knew she could face the future with Zack at her side.

"Miss Winter?" A man in surgical scrubs came from the double doors.

"Yes?" She jumped up. Zack stood and together they walked to the doctor. He reached out to clasp her hand, squeezing it slightly to give her courage.

"Your father did fine. He's in recovery, will be back in his room in another hour or so. You can see him then, for a few minutes. He'll probably sleep through the night, but should be ready for visitors in the morning."

"Thank you," she said, reaching out to shake his hand. "Thank you."

Once he left, Marcie turned to Zack. "I'm so relieved."

"Thank you, Father, for the blessing of this successful surgery. We pray for a speedy recovery for Marcie's dad. May the family who donated this kidney be comforted knowing it's giving life to another," Zack said softly, folding her into his arms while she released tension with tears.

Zack and Marcie waited until they could see Bill after he awoke in recovery. He was still groggy and tired, and insisted Marcie go back home and get some rest.

"I'll sleep all night, so you go home and do the same," he grumbled, his eyes closing.

"I hate to be so far away."

"I'm in God's hands, you can't get better than that. Come back tomorrow—but not too early," he said, almost asleep again.

She kissed her father and then joined Zack. Soon they were speeding toward Rocky Point.

"It's a miracle a kidney was found so soon," she mused as the trees whizzed by.

"God's still making miracles," Zack said, reaching out to take her hand. "He let you and me come back together, didn't He?"

She nodded, squeezing his hand slightly, contentment spreading. She closed her eyes in silent prayer and soon fell asleep, the stress of the day catching up with her.

Zack drove through the night, almost unable to believe Marcie had said she loved him. He didn't deserve it. He also didn't deserve the grace from God, but he knew it was there. He would spend the rest of his days proving he could be depended upon and would always be there for her. He offered a quiet prayer of thanks for so many things.

When they reached her apartment, he woke her.

"You're home. Do as your father said and get a good night's rest."

"Sorry I conked out on you. I think it was the relief of knowing things are going to be okay with my dad."

"Don't worry about that. I'll see you in the morning." He walked her to her door and gave her a lingering kiss before turning and running down the steps.

The next morning Marcie headed to the café early, to check in on everything, update her employees and make plans to be at the hospital for the next few days.

She was about to leave for Portland when Zack entered the kitchen, looking for her.

"I stopped by your apartment first, and when

there was no answer, I tried here," he said, waving to the kitchen staff as he entered Marcie's office.

"I'm just winding up things so I can get back up to Portland. I spoke to my dad, and he's feeling sore and tired, but otherwise is happy."

"I'll drive you up," Zack said.

She smiled as she nodded. "I'd like that."

When they left Rocky Point, Zack detoured to drive by the Kincaid residence.

"Did you forget something?" she asked when he pulled into the driveway.

"You could say that." He stopped and got out to go around and open the passenger door.

"Come with me for a couple of minutes."

She got out, looking at the house, freshly painted and surrounded by the partially painted picket fence. He didn't stop, but walked around the fence and headed for the bluff. Curious, Marcie followed until they stood at the edge, the blue Atlantic stretching out as far as the eye could see.

"I'm hoping this is right," he said nervously.

"What?"

"The house by the sea. I'm buying out Joe's half. And the picket fence. And the time and the place." Turning, he took her hands in his and looked into her eyes. "Marcie, would you marry me?"

Slowly she smiled, happiness and delight flooding through her. "Yes, Zack, I'd be most honored."

With a whoop of joy, he picked her up and spun

them around. "Thank you, Lord!" he shouted. She laughed with happiness. God did perform miracles. All fear for their future was gone. She would trust in God and Zack from now on and knew, this time around, when the wedding ceremony started Zack would be waiting for her to walk up the aisle to bind her life with his.

They had plans to make, people to tell. It was agreed between them to tell Joe and Gillian first. Suddenly what Gillian said earlier made sense. She'd known Zack was buying the house and fixing it up. No wonder she'd been so sure his return home was permanent.

"Unless you think we should tell your father first," he said.

"Maybe we'll wait on that, until he's better."

"I can see your point. Do you think he'll forgive me one day?"

"When he sees how happy I am, you can be sure he will. But we need to tell Joe before he guesses," she said. "But I don't want to take away from their wedding." She was almost giddy with happiness, warring with her continued concern about her father.

"I think my brother suspects I was going this direction. I think he'll be pleased. And I think our happiness will make theirs even more so."

"Now I'll really be Jenny's aunt. She's called me that all along, as an honorary title."

"Two things we need to talk about," he said slowly. "First—I need to go back to Paris to close down my apartment, ship home some things, sell my car. I can wait and we can make it a honeymoon trip if you like."

"Paris for a honeymoon, you're kidding. Of course I'd like!"

"Okay. Next, I'm not sure I'm going into partnership with Joe. I mean, I might, but not halves. I really like the idea of the training course for teen drivers. I've been looking into different programs to learn more about it. I think I want to do something along those lines. What do you think?"

"I think that's wonderful. When I remember how Sean was before you took an interest, and seeing him now, it's amazing. Boys especially need good male role models. And when there's no father in the picture, who can they turn to? You surprise me, though."

"I remember my dad, he was pretty great. If I can offer half what he did to boys who don't have a father, I'd be satisfied."

"So, knowing the plans I have, and the fact nothing will mean anything if you're not there with me, I want to marry you in the worst way. I've missed you every day since I left. I love you, Marcie Winter, I always have. This time I'll stand by, no matter what."

"I love you, Zack Kincaid, I always have. And I'm counting on you."

He smiled as he drew her close for a kiss to seal the vows. No matter what the future held, love and faith would see them through.

* * * * *

Dear Reader,

One stayed, one left. Has that happened to you? Marcie Winter has always loved Rocky Point, Maine, where she was born and raised. All she ever wanted was to build a life in the town, raise a family and know everyone in town. Her family has been in Rocky Point for generations. She saw no reason to be the one to leave.

Zack Kincaid wanted adventure and excitement—more than would ever be found in a small coastal town in Maine. While he was growing up, he yearned for more than the fishing village offered. When the call for adventure arrived, the timing was bad. But he took it anyway, and broke Marcie's heart.

A life-changing event years later, however, has Zack examining if choices made at eighteen were to last all his life. Maybe it was time to reevaluate decisions, see what life had to offer surrounded by family and life-long friends. So back to Rocky Point he goes when he learns of his brother's injuries. Getting to know his brother better, his niece, reconnecting with old friends has Zack viewing life in the small town differently. He's seen the bigger world, but in Rocky Point feels a tie that can't be denied.

Plus, there's the girl he left behind.

The past can't be recaptured. But sometimes the future can be even brighter.

I hope you enjoy the journey Zack and Marcie make.

All the best,

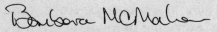

Barbara McMahan

QUESTIONS FOR DISCUSSION

1. The story opens with Marcie confronting the man she had one time thought to marry. Do you think her reactions were appropriate? Has anything like that ever happened to you or someone you know? How did they handle a meeting years later?

2. As Zack put it, their families had been in Rocky Point since the 1700s. He'd felt stifled by the small town and the history. He wanted to see bright lights and more exciting locations. Are you more like Zack, or Marcie, who loved her town and wanted to stay put? After the initial choice, did you ever think about the other path not chosen?

3. A teenager approaches Zack to ask about racing pointers. Do you feel Zack's response was appropriate? Would you have expected him to ignore the teen or do more?

4. Zack seems repentant about his leaving. Do you think it is a recent emotion? If leaving someone behind happened to you, would you want to discuss it or say it was over and done with and

move on? Is Marcie's reaction similar to one you'd have if you were the one left behind?

5. Marcie takes her father for granted, then suddenly notices he looks older than she expects. Is that a common occurrence—people are so involved with their own lives they lose touch with what's going on with parents or siblings? What could Marcie have done to keep up on what was going on with her father?

6. When Zack tentatively mentions plans for a car track to the sheriff, Tate immediately thinks of a place that might work. Do you think that was coincidence or part of a greater plan God had for Zack—the work he might do with teenagers?

7. When Zack learns of the car problem Marcie's father has, he goes to offer to look at it for the man. His reception is less than cordial. Do you think his motives were purely to repair the car, or to also try to regain trust and friendship with the father of the woman he is interested in? Does it matter if the job gets done?

8. What do you think of Gillian's plans to have such a wide range of attendants for her wedding, from a ninety-three-year-old to a seven-

year-old? Have you attended weddings with such a wide range? How did you feel?

9. No one seems to take Zack seriously when he says he wants to remain in Rocky Point. At one point he says he isn't going to say it again. Is that what you would have done? Waited for people to have faith in what you say, or keep saying it? Do you think he really meant it from the first, or did the conviction grow the longer he stayed?

10. Zack goes from a pleasant afternoon on the beach with his niece to a call from his manager pressing him to return. He says he wants to stay in Rocky Point, but the lure of the glamour of his job and the exotic places he's visited returns. Do you think that was a kind of testing to make sure he knew what he was choosing?

11. When Sean gets into trouble, he calls Zack. He goes to help out and suddenly realizes he's doing what his father did a time or two. It's a turning point in leaving childhood and recognizing he's an adult. Does he handle it well?

12. Despite being wary around Zack, Marcie accepts invitations he gives—to chaperone the girls on a cookout, to go to the old factory to

check out the parking lot. Does she give in to her curiosity too easily? Is she really trying to see him as he is now and not recapture the past they once shared?

13. Marcie's dad doesn't reveal his health situation, trying to protect his only child even though she's a capable adult. Do you think that was wise? Were you surprised to have him hide the truth? How do you think Marcie felt when she learned the full situation?

14. Zack agrees to race again. Why do you think he really chooses to do that? Would you have felt betrayed if he'd told you over and over he was staying and then left? Would you expect him back?

15. Do you think Zack's return to faith is a major reason he makes the offer of a transplant that he does? Do you think it had an effect on Marcie's falling in love with him again? Do you feel the rest of their lives would be enhanced by putting God in the center of their marriage?

LARGER-PRINT BOOKS!

GET 2 FREE
LARGER-PRINT NOVELS
PLUS 2 FREE
MYSTERY GIFTS

Larger-print novels are now available...

YES! Please send me 2 FREE LARGER-PRINT Love Inspired® novels and my 2 FREE mystery gifts (gifts are worth about $10). After receiving them, if I don't wish to receive any more books, I can return the shipping statement marked "cancel". If I don't cancel, I will receive 6 brand-new novels every month and be billed just $4.74 per book in the U.S. or $5.24 per book in Canada. That's a saving of at least 24% off the cover price. It's quite a bargain! Shipping and handling is just 50¢ per book in the U.S. and 75¢ per book in Canada.* I understand that accepting the 2 free books and gifts places me under no obligation to buy anything. I can always return a shipment and cancel at any time. Even if I never buy another book, the two free books and gifts are mine to keep forever.

122/322 IDN FC79

Name _____ (PLEASE PRINT) _____

Address _____ Apt. # _____

City _____ State/Prov. _____ Zip/Postal Code _____

Signature (if under 18, a parent or guardian must sign)

Mail to the **Reader Service:**
IN U.S.A.: P.O. Box 1867, Buffalo, NY 14240-1867
IN CANADA: P.O. Box 609, Fort Erie, Ontario L2A 5X3

Not valid to current subscribers to Love Inspired Larger-Print books.

**Are you a current subscriber to Love Inspired books
and want to receive the larger-print edition?
Call 1-800-873-8635 or visit www.ReaderService.com.**

* Terms and prices subject to change without notice. Prices do not include applicable taxes. Sales tax applicable in N.Y. Canadian residents will be charged applicable taxes. Offer not valid in Quebec. This offer is limited to one order per household. All orders subject to credit approval. Credit or debit balances in a customer's account(s) may be offset by any other outstanding balance owed by or to the customer. Please allow 4 to 6 weeks for delivery. Offer available while quantities last.

Your Privacy—The Reader Service is committed to protecting your privacy. Our Privacy Policy is available online at www.ReaderService.com or upon request from the Reader Service.

We make a portion of our mailing list available to reputable third parties that offer products we believe may interest you. If you prefer that we not exchange your name with third parties, or if you wish to clarify or modify your communication preferences, please visit us at www.ReaderService.com/consumerchoice or write to us at Reader Service Preference Service, P.O. Box 9062, Buffalo, NY 14269. Include your complete name and address.

LILPI I